SUSAN SCARLETT
LOVE IN A MIST

SUSAN Scarlett is a pseudonym of the author Noel Streatfeild (1895-1986). She was born in Sussex, England, the second of five surviving children of William Champion Streatfeild, later the Bishop of Lewes, and Janet Venn. As a child she showed an interest in acting, and upon reaching adulthood sought a career in theatre, which she pursued for ten years, in addition to modelling. Her familiarity with the stage was the basis for many of her popular books.

Her first children's book was *Ballet Shoes* (1936), which launched a successful career writing for children. In addition to children's books and memoirs, she also wrote fiction for adults, including romantic novels under the name 'Susan Scarlett'. The twelve Susan Scarlett novels are now republished by Dean Street Press.

Noel Streatfeild was appointed an Officer of the Order of the British Empire (OBE) in 1983.

ADULT FICTION BY NOEL STREATFEILD

As Noel Streatfeild

The Whicharts (1931)

Parson's Nine (1932)

Tops and Bottoms (1933)

A Shepherdess of Sheep (1934)

It Pays to be Good (1936)

Caroline England (1937)

Luke (1939)

The Winter is Past (1940)

I Ordered a Table for Six (1942)

Myra Carroll (1944)

Saplings (1945)

Grass in Piccadilly (1947)

Mothering Sunday (1950)

Aunt Clara (1952)

Judith (1956)

The Silent Speaker (1961)

As Susan Scarlett
(All available from Dean Street Press)

Clothes-Pegs (1939)

Sally-Ann (1939)

Peter and Paul (1940)

Ten Way Street (1940)

The Man in the Dark (1940)

Babbacombe's (1941)

Under the Rainbow (1942)

Summer Pudding (1943)

Murder While You Work (1944)

Poppies for England (1948)

Pirouette (1948)

Love in a Mist (1951)

SUSAN SCARLETT

LOVE IN A MIST

With an introduction
by Elizabeth Crawford

DEAN STREET PRESS

When reviewing *Clothes-Pegs*, Susan Scarlett's first novel, the *Nottingham Journal* (4 April 1939) praised the 'clean, clear atmosphere carefully produced by a writer who shows a rich experience in her writing and a charm which should make this first effort in the realm of the novel the forerunner of other attractive works'. Other reviewers, however, appeared alert to the fact that *Clothes-Pegs* was not the work of a tyro novelist but one whom *The Hastings & St Leonards Observer* (4 February 1939) described as 'already well-known', while explaining that this 'bright, clear, generous work', was 'her first novel of this type'. It is possible that the reviewer for this paper had some knowledge of the true identity of the author for, under her real name, Noel Streatfeild had, as the daughter of the one-time vicar of St Peter's Church in St Leonards, featured in its pages on a number of occasions.

By the time she was reincarnated as 'Susan Scarlett', Noel Streatfeild (1897-1986) had published six novels for adults and three for children, one of which had recently won the prestigious Carnegie Medal. Under her own name she continued publishing for another 40 years, while Susan Scarlett had a briefer existence, never acknowledged by her only begetter. Having found the story easy to write, Noel Streatfeild had thought little of *Ballet Shoes*, her acclaimed first novel for children, and, similarly, may have felt Susan Scarlett too facile a writer with whom to be identified. For Susan Scarlett's stories were, as the *Daily Telegraph* (24 February 1939) wrote of *Clothes-Pegs*, 'definitely unreal, delightfully impossible'. They were fairy tales, with realistic backgrounds, categorised as perfect 'reading for Black-out nights' for the 'lady of the house' (*Aberdeen Press and Journal*, 16 October 1939). As Susan Scarlett, Noel Streatfeild was able to offer daydreams to her readers, exploiting her varied experiences and interests to create, as her publisher advertised, 'light, bright, brilliant present-day romances'.

Noel Streatfeild was the second of the four surviving children of parents who had inherited upper-middle class values and expectations without, on a clergy salary, the financial means of realising them. Rebellious and extrovert, in her childhood and youth she had found many aspects of vicarage life unappealing, resenting both the restrictions thought necessary to ensure that a vicar's daughter behaved in a manner appropriate to the family's status, and the genteel impecuniousness and unworldliness that deprived her of, in particular, the finer clothes she craved. Her lack of scholarly application had unfitted her for any suitable occupation, but, after the end of the First World War, during which she spent time as a volunteer nurse and as a munition worker, she did persuade her parents to let her realise her dream of becoming an actress. Her stage career, which lasted ten years, was not totally unsuccessful but, as she was to describe on *Desert Island Discs*, it was while passing the Great Barrier Reef on her return from an Australian theatrical tour that she decided she had little future as an actress and would, instead, become a writer. A necessary sense of discipline having been instilled in her by life both in the vicarage and on the stage, she set to work and in 1931 produced *The Whicharts*, a creditable first novel.

By 1937 Noel was turning her thoughts towards Hollywood, with the hope of gaining work as a scriptwriter, and sometime that year, before setting sail for what proved to be a short, unfruitful trip, she entered, as 'Susan Scarlett', into a contract with the publishing firm of Hodder and Stoughton. The advance of £50 she received, against a novel entitled *Peter and Paul*, may even have helped finance her visit. However, the Hodder costing ledger makes clear that this novel was not delivered when expected, so that in January 1939 it was with *Clothes-Pegs* that Susan Scarlett made her debut. For both this and *Peter and Paul* (January 1940) Noel drew on her experience of occasional employment as a model in a fashion house, work for which, as she later explained, tall, thin actresses were much in demand in the 1920s.

Both *Clothes-Pegs* and *Peter and Paul* have as their settings Mayfair modiste establishments (Hanover Square and Bruton Street respectively), while the second Susan Scarlett novel, *Sally-Ann* (October 1939) is set in a beauty salon in nearby Dover Street. Noel was clearly familiar with establishments such as this, having, under her stage name 'Noelle Sonning', been photographed to advertise in *The Sphere* (22 November 1924) the skills of M. Emile of Conduit Street who had 'strongly waved and fluffed her hair to give a "bobbed" effect'. *Sally-Ann* and *Clothes-Pegs* both feature a lovely, young, lower-class 'Cinderella', who, despite living with her family in, respectively, Chelsea (the rougher part) and suburban 'Coulsden' (by which may, or may not, be meant Coulsdon in the Croydon area, south of London), meets, through her Mayfair employment, an upper-class 'Prince Charming'. The theme is varied in *Peter and Paul* for, in this case, twins

Pauline and Petronella are, in the words of the reviewer in the *Birmingham Gazette* (5 February 1940), 'launched into the world with jobs in a London fashion shop after a childhood hedged, as it were, by the vicarage privet'. As we have seen, the trajectory from staid vicarage to glamorous Mayfair, with, for one twin, a further move onwards to Hollywood, was to have been the subject of Susan Scarlett's debut, but perhaps it was felt that her initial readership might more readily identify with a heroine who began the journey to a fairy-tale destiny from an address such as '110 Mercia Lane, Coulsden'.

As the privations of war began to take effect, Susan Scarlett ensured that her readers were supplied with ample and loving descriptions of the worldly goods that were becoming all but unobtainable. The novels revel in all forms of dress, from underwear, 'sheer triple ninon step-ins, cut on the cross, so that they fitted like a glove' (*Clothes-Pegs*), through daywear, 'The frock was blue. The colour of harebells. Made of some silk and wool material. It had perfect cut.' (*Peter and Paul*), to costumes, such as 'a brocaded evening coat; it was almost military in cut, with squared shoulders and a little tailored collar, very tailored at the waist, where it went in to flare out to the floor' (*Sally-Ann*), suitable to wear while dining at the Berkeley or the Ivy, establishments to which her heroines – and her readers – were introduced. Such details and the satisfying plots, in which innocent loveliness triumphs against the machinations of Society beauties, did indeed prove popular. Initial print runs of 2000 or 2500 soon sold out and reprints and cheaper editions were ordered. For instance, by the time it went out of print at the end of 1943, *Clothes-Pegs* had sold a total of

13,500 copies, providing welcome royalties for Noel and a definite profit for Hodder.

Susan Scarlett novels appeared in quick succession, particularly in the early years of the war, promoted to readers as a brand; 'You enjoyed *Clothes-Pegs*. You will love Susan Scarlett's *Sally-Ann*', ran an advertisement in the *Observer* (5 November 1939). Both *Sally-Ann* and a fourth novel, *Ten Way Street* (1940), published barely five months after *Peter and Paul*, reached a hitherto untapped audience, each being serialised daily in the *Dundee Courier*. It is thought that others of the twelve Susan Scarlett novels appeared as serials in women's magazines, but it has proved possible to identify only one, her eleventh, *Pirouette*, which appeared, lusciously illustrated, in *Woman* in January and February 1948, some months before its book publication. In this novel, trailed as 'An enthralling story – set against the glittering fairyland background of the ballet', Susan Scarlett benefited from Noel Streatfeild's knowledge of the world of dance, while giving her post-war readers a young heroine who chose a husband over a promising career. For, common to most of the Susan Scarlett novels is the fact that the central figure is, before falling into the arms of her 'Prince Charming', a worker, whether, as we have seen, a Mayfair mannequin or beauty specialist, or a children's nanny, 'trained' in *Ten Way Street*, or, as in *Under the Rainbow* (1942), the untrained minder of vicarage orphans; in *The Man in the Dark* (1941) a paid companion to a blinded motor car racer; in *Babbacombe's* (1941) a department store assistant; in *Murder While You Work* (1944) a munition worker; in *Poppies for England* (1948) a member of a concert party; or, in *Pirouette*, a ballet dancer. There are only two exceptions, the first being the heroine of *Summer Pudding* (1943) who, bombed out of the London office in which she worked, has been forced to retreat to an archetypal southern English village. The other is *Love in a Mist* (1951), the final Susan Scarlett novel, in which, with the zeitgeist returning women to hearth and home, the central character is a housewife and mother, albeit one, an American, who, prompted by a too-earnest interest in child psychology, popular in the post-war years, attempts to cure what she perceives as her four-year-old son's neuroses with the rather radical treatment of film stardom.

Between 1938 and 1951, while writing as Susan Scarlett, Noel Streatfeild also published a dozen or so novels under her own name, some for children, some for adults. This was despite having no permanent home after 1941 when her flat was bombed, and while undertaking arduous volunteer work, both as an air raid warden close to home in Mayfair, and as a provider of tea and sympathy in an impoverished area of south-east London. Susan Scarlett certainly helped with Noel's expenses over this period, garnering, for instance, an advance of £300 for *Love in a Mist*. Although there were to be no new Susan Scarlett novels, in the 1950s Hodder reissued cheap editions of *Babbacombe's*, *Pirouette*, and *Under the Rainbow*, the 60,000 copies of the latter only finally exhausted in 1959.

During the 'Susan Scarlett' years, some of the darkest of the 20th century, the adjectives applied most commonly to her novels were 'light' and 'bright'. While immersed in a Susan Scarlett novel her readers, whether book buyers or library borrowers, were able momentarily to forget their everyday cares and suspend disbelief, for as the reviewer in the *Daily Telegraph* (8 February 1941) declared, 'Miss Scarlett has a way with her; she makes us accept the most unlikely things'.

Elizabeth Crawford

CHAPTER 1
Meet the Trings

Ruth sucked the end of her pen. A passer-by might have thought she was looking at her garden. It was worth looking at, with its crocuses, scyllas, and its prunus-tree rosetted with flowers, saying, "You won't believe it but spring is on the way". Or the passer-by might have thought she was looking at the High Street. Not that she could see much of it, because most of it was hidden behind the laurel hedge, so her only glimpse of it was over the neat, low, green gate. But in either case the passer-by would have been wrong. Ruth's eyes were looking at another house and another street, neither of which had she seen for over five years.

Ruth could see her home as clearly as though it were outside her window. The small, boxy frame-house lay back from the street, but it was not shut in by a hedge or wall as in England; it lay open to all eyes, surrounded by a square of grass. Right now there would be no flowers, it would be still winter. Illinois had real seasons; often the weather behaved strangely, but winter was winter and summer was summer there. In England you never knew what to expect; it could be the same warm temperature at the end of winter as it would be in the spring, or even, if it came to that, as it would be in June; then suddenly it would turn cold, like to-day, not cold as it was at home, but this damp cold which ate into your bones. What would be the time at home now? Well past midnight, she reckoned. Father and Mother would be in bed and asleep. She peered into their bedroom. "You will never believe it, Ruthie," her mother had written, "but I have got my new drapes and spread at last, and just what I wanted. I told your father we could not afford them right now, but he said that as all you children were married he reckoned it was time we gave ourselves a little fun." Ruth saw just how those new chintz curtains and that bedspread looked; how often she had heard her mother say because you lived in a city there was no reason for your home to look that way; you could fix a country-homesy look any place. Someone passed the gate. The movement brought Ruth's eyes back from Illinois. She looked at her pen and the sheets of notepaper before her. Her letter was partly written, but there was still a lot of space to fill. One of the worst things about marrying a foreigner and living the other side of the world was that little by little as the years passed there was less to write home about. When she had first married Peter she had not found time to write all there had been to say. There had been the house to describe; as she wrote those early letters she could hear her mother's deep laugh as she read paragraphs out loud; how she would have told the neighbours that Ruthie's home, though it was right on Main Street and quite a little place, was called "Clovelly". She had known then, as her pen raced over the pages, how her family were enjoying her descriptions of the queer fixings, especially her description of the bath-fixings, with the geyser which was out of this world. Letters from home still asked after the geyser, which was still there, but Ruth did not find it funny any more. Her family had met Peter, but there had been Peter's family to describe. What fun it had been trying to draw word-pictures of Mum and Dad-Tring. Mum-Tring shopping with a string bag. Mum-Tring giving herself a treat meeting friends in in order to drink a cup of the most terrible coffee in what was called a teashop. Mum-Tring going to a whist drive. They had been superficial pictures, of course; Ruth was far too intelligent to think you could understand in-laws, especially foreign in-laws, in a few months, and her father and mother would have been certain to criticise her had they thought she was trying to do so. It had been difficult to draw even a superficial picture of Dad-Tring; neither his business nor his position had quite their counterparts back home. Peter, when he had visited at her home, had described the family business as a small store. So it was, but he had not explained he was the fourth generation to work there, that it had started as a little grocer's shop and had grown into a big grocery where the rich had called first in horse-drawn carriages and later in automobiles and had given their orders to Peter's grandfather or great-grandfather, who came out on to the sidewalk wearing white aprons, to write them down. At some time a fruit, vegetable and flower department had been added, and that too sold nothing but the best and most expensive. It was not a luxury store when Ruth had seen it. The war had swept away most of those sort of goods, but Tring's stocked any luxuries that were to be had, and when anyone wanted something special they would say, "I shall try Tring's." In describing Tring's Ruth had never attempted to describe Dad-Tring's attitude to his customers. Sometimes she happened to be in the shop as he was serving some, often shabby, man or woman without much money to spend. When they had gone he would say to her in a voice warm with love and respect, "That was one of our old customers, Ruth." Nor had she the words to describe the position between Dad-Tring and the old customers. He called them "M'Lord", "M'Lady", "Sir", "Madam", yet they seemed old friends. What he called them appeared to make no odds to Dad-Tring's position; it seemed he kept his dignity and the customers kept theirs. Put on paper this sounded the sort of class distinction and snootiness you read about in Britain, but it was not like that really; it just seemed it was something the British understood and liked and saw no reason to alter.

Neither could she explain Dad-Tring's position in the town. Ruth had always thought she knew what a mayor was, but a mayor in England was not a mayor as she understood mayors. They were less important somehow and yet more important, or rather, important in a different way—anyway, you couldn't explain all that in a letter. She just wrote that Dad-Tring had been mayor three times, and let her family make what they liked of the statement. Nor could you explain in a letter that "fun" was not a word people like the Trings knew anything about. The Trings too were now on their own, for their boys were married, but Dad-Tring would never say, as her father had done, that it was time he and Mum-Tring had fun.

When Ruth had first married she had covered pages describing Dad and Mum-Tring's furnishings: the heavy old-fashioned furniture; the heavy, dull, dust-laden curtains; the fly-walked scriptural engravings. She wished now she had never written those letters; her family had enjoyed her descriptions so much and were always asking for further news. Had Mr. and Mrs. Tring had their bedroom made over yet? Surely they had not still got those simply terrible pictures? In five years Ruth had learnt that Dad and Mum-Tring would never "make over" any room. They were quite satisfied with their home as it was.

Ruth looked at her pen—how lovely to be able to relax and pour out to her mother all her pent-up feelings! Explain to that wise, all-loving mother that though she still adored Peter, his satisfaction in going on the same way year in and year out was getting her down. That although she wrote happily, everything was not as happy as it sounded; especially she was anxious about little Paul. He was as lovely as his photographs, and so smart he just left every other four-year-old (except his cousin Jimmie, who was too clever to live) way on the skyline. But, since he was so smart, did not her mother think it crazy to make a settled plan that he went to work at Tring's? Did she not think a boy like Paul ought to feel free to get any place? She would like to have talked to her mother to explain that she could not make Peter see this, how he laughed and said Paul was lucky to have a business to fall into. Why, he even denied that Paul was particularly smart. Then there was yesterday. It was yesterday that made it so difficult to write. Paul did have bad-tempered fits. It just seemed he had to be the centre of everything, and if he was not he got one of his difficult turns, screaming, drumming his heels on the floor, and—which terrified her—holding his breath. Peter had not seen one of these turns, as they mostly happened when he was out working, but yesterday being a Sunday, he was home.

There had been two little friends to tea with Paul, and in some game there was argument and he got the worst of it. Peter at the first scream had said firmly, "Shut up, Paul." Paul, far from shutting up, had thrown himself on the floor screaming at the top of his voice, drumming the carpet with his heels. Peter had got up. "Shut up, Paul, or . . ." Ruth had caught at his arm and whispered, "Be careful, Peter, or he'll maybe hold his breath." Paul possibly had overheard this; anyway, he had immediately held his breath. In terror Ruth had watched his face turn puce-coloured. Peter had not stayed to watch what had happened; he had run out of the room and in a moment was back with a jug of cold water, which he had thrown straight into Paul's face. It had made the child retrieve his breath, and before he could hold it again Peter had said, "Get up, and take off that wet shirt." Paul had taken a deep breath to let out another scream; before it came Peter had added, "There's plenty more cold water in the tap, but I don't intend to waste my Sunday afternoon carrying it to you; if you want to scream any more you can do it in the bathroom, where the water is handy."

Paul had not screamed any more—he had in fact behaved for the rest of the day like a little angel, but Ruth had not been happy about him. He had seemed to her more reserved than customary, and though he had hugged her when she had put him to bed, she was sure it was a less bear-like hug than he usually gave her. Very worried, she returned to the living-room determined to have it out with Peter.

Peter was sitting by the living-room fire smoking his pipe and reading a paper; she had not interrupted him—which she knew he loathed—but had settled quietly opposite him, darning one of Paul's socks. Presently Peter had put his paper down to discuss some piece of news he had been reading. As he lowered the paper the light of the lamp fell on his head. It made his fair hair blaze, as if the sun was shining on a field of corn. He had told her what had interested him in the paper, and as he spoke, his blue eyes on hers, she felt the same weakness and softness she had felt the first time she had ever seen him. On his father's advice Peter had spent his war gratuity visiting America, attached to some organisation which was sent over to study American business methods. She could still hear the buzzer which called her to Mr. Sholtz's office, and the tone of Mr. Sholtz's' voice explaining to a roomful of men that this was his stenographer, Miss Ruth Russell, who would fix up for them they saw everything they wished to see. But her eyes, while Mr. Sholtz spoke, had been on Peter, and in that second, though she had not realised it at the time, she had given him her heart. Last night, as he had looked at her, she had wanted to listen, smile and be cosy, she had not wanted to spoil things by an argument, but she had quickly pulled herself together; that was no way to feel; she was a mother and she must protect her child.

"I am not happy about little Paul. I do not feel you used the right method this afternoon. I recognise that in some ways he is ill-adjusted, but we want to get down to the cause and straighten it out. I feel throwing water on him, shaming him before his little friends, may have done him harm deep down."

Peter had first stared at her puzzled, then he had thrown back his head and roared with laughter.

"Darling, you are a scream when you talk like that! Ill-adjusted! He's just spoilt. He was lucky I didn't take a slipper to him."

It had been their first quarrel which had its roots in incompatible views. Backward and forward the argument went, Peter getting rather cross and inclined to shout,

Ruth holding on to her temper, keeping her voice down and her replies reasoned. The striking of the clock had finished the argument, for Ruth had to get supper.

In her kitchen Ruth had tried to be just. She knew she was in the right. Paul was wrongly adjusted and maybe an introvert, but there were people trained to straighten children out, and terrible harm, could come from wrong treatment. But, she must not be unfair to Peter. The British were backward about mental conditions, they knew very little about exceptional children and their emotional problems; compared to America, psychiatric treatment was in its infancy. Peter (and she suspected he was not unique) thought the word "psychologist" funny, and used only by professional comedians. It was no good rushing matters. A happy home was of as much importance to little Paul as the straightening out of his emotional problems. As she arranged the salad and fixed the main dish, Ruth decided that it would be tactful to let the subject of Paul die for that night. She thought she knew just how Peter would be feeling; he might not know what she had been talking about, but he hated her to be upset. Before when they had quarrelled about something he had not rested until he was sure everything was smoothed out. As she put their supper on a tray she deliberately smiled. She knew Peter; he would be hoping for that smile. It was a nice supper; she did not want it spoilt for him by any friction.

Peter had not been waiting for her smile. He was once more deep in his newspaper. Seeing this, Ruth's smile had died, and it was his cheerful grin which greeted her.

"Just listen to this, darling . . ." As if there had been no vital argument about Paul, he read her something quite irrelevant from his paper.

Thinking of that supper, Ruth was surprised and thankful she had managed to hold her tongue. It would have been so easy to have let herself get really upset, which would have been foolish. Dad and Mum-Tring would call in, as they usually did on their way back from evening church, and the last thing that she wished was that they should feel anything was wrong between her and Peter. If they had heard what the argument was about they would have been sure to take sides with Peter, not because it was their custom to agree with their son, but because they just did not know what psychiatry was. They would have done their best not to seem to favour Peter, because they went out of their way to be sweet to her, but over the question of Paul they could not have helped themselves. Dad-Tring, as like as not, would have quoted those maddening lines about sparing the rod and spoiling the child. As it was, because she said nothing, Dad and Mum-Tring turned up and stayed quite a while, and ate some little cheese canapés she had made, and they had a nice talk about nothing at all, and went home happy, not knowing anything was wrong. But it was not only Mum and Dad-Tring who had not known that anything was wrong; Peter seemed to have forgotten there had ever been an argument.

Ruth had not intended to let the day finish that way. They had gone to bed soon after Mum and Dad-Tring had left, and in the darkness with his arms round her and her cheek against his she had tried again.

"Peter, will you listen now, without being cross, if I explain to you some of the difficulties which I think Paul—"

She had got no further. Peter had kissed her.

"You may not. The little tough's had you all day. I want you now."

Ruth looked down at her letter; how easy it would be to talk about Paul to her mother, but how difficult to explain on paper. On paper what you said had a finality. She could hear her mother say to her father, "Ruth's worried about Paul. She writes he needs psychiatric treatment." In words it would not be nearly as definite as that. She would describe the scene and what had happened, and her mother, rocking herself to and fro in her old chair, would listen, and not only advise but would leave her feeling quite different. Mother had that way with troubles. She never belittled them, but she kind of ironed them out.

Emma Tring walked slowly towards "Clovelly". Because there was rain or perhaps sleet about, she was wearing her macintosh; she disliked wearing her macintosh when it was cold, as it was hard to keep warm in it, whereas it was easy to keep warm in her thick cloth coat. But Emma had been brought up to wear a macintosh when it was damp, so, though there was no one in the house to insist that she did so, she wore a macintosh. She hated an umbrella when shopping—it bumped into people and was hard to handle, when as well she had her handbag and her string shopping-bag—but she had always used an umbrella when it was wet, and so would continue to use an umbrella. As she neared "Clovelly", in spite of longing to get under cover out of the cold, she walked more slowly. She went over in her mind what she was going to say. She would give Ruth the packet of breakfast food right away. She had been lucky to see that packet of Ruth's favourite cereal that very morning; it was hard to get and she was sure she would be pleased. It made a nice excuse for dropping in. Once she had given Ruth the breakfast food she would have to chance what came next; perhaps Ruth would give her a cup of that lovely coffee she made. That would be nice and warming, and it was so much easier to talk with a cup in your hand. She must keep a guard on herself. Not by a lifted eyebrow must Ruth know that she knew anything was wrong last night. It was only because Ruth was so extraordinarily easy to talk to that she had sensed anything was the matter; Dad had not noticed anything, but, then, he had talked mainly to Peter, and Peter had been entirely himself. Whatever had upset Ruth had not upset Peter; but, then, that was the Trings all over. When she had first married and the boys had been growing up there had been a number of times when she had cried her eyes out over something, and Dad had not known anything was wrong. Of course she might not get the opportunity to let Ruth know that she knew just how blind and stubborn a Tring could be, but it was worth coming out in the cold and the wet just on the chance. Emma took it for granted that Ruth thought her dowdy and old-fashioned, and she thought it natural that she should, seeing how clever she was and how smart and pretty she always looked. She did not hope that Ruth would ever come to treat her as a friend and talk things out with her; why should she? Ruth, so modern and quick-witted, would be unlikely to get any help from talking to her. But it might assist the girl to know that her mother-in-law was not the sort to think that any trouble in the home must come from the daughter-in-law, because her son could never be in the wrong. She had married a Tring, had a Tring father-in-law and borne three Tring sons and knew differently.

Ruth heard the gate click. She was surprised to see Mum-Tring, who seldom called in the morning. She ran to open the front door.

"Why, Mum, whatever has brought you out on a morning like this? Come right in and sit by the fire. I'll have a cup of coffee ready for us in two minutes. You must need it. I do despise this weather, don't you?"

Emma sat by the fire. She looked admiringly at Ruth. How neat and shining her hair was! That short cut suited her, though when it was first cut she had thought it was a pity to clip off any of her red-brown curls. She watched Ruth tie an apron over her blue dress. She herself always wore a serviceable overall when she was working, but she thought Ruth's aprons charming. Ruth had made her several for birthdays and Christmas, but though she pretended to wear them, hanging each in turn on her kitchen door, she never did. She felt silly in the dainty frilled things; whatever would people think who saw her got up in one? They would very likely say she fancied herself, and would talk about it and she would be laughed at.

Ruth, with an ease which had never ceased to amaze Emma, came in with a beautifully set out tray of coffee and a plate of what she called crackers, but to Emma were biscuits. Emma had learnt many things from Ruth, and setting out a tray prettily for unexpected guests was one of them, but her trays never looked as Ruth's trays looked and they were never produced with Ruth's careless ease. She had once made the mistake of remarking on this to her two other daughters-in-law, Anna and Doris, and had been thoroughly snubbed. Anna, her eldest son George's wife, had said in her cool, to Emma, terribly BBC voice, "Nothing odd in that. Anybody can do it if they are brought up to it. But people who have been brought up to be waited on, and find themselves almost without help, have no time for that sort of nonsense." Doris, Andrew's wife, the clever one of the family, had added: "Anyone could manage nice snacks if they had the run of Ruth's food-parcels." Emma had not agreed with Anna and Doris, she seldom did, and continued to admire Ruth's way with a tray.

Emma took the packet of breakfast food from her string bag, her eyes twinkled.

"You mustn't tell Peter or Dad, but I bought it at Johnson's. You can often get things there which you can't get at Tring's. Dad doesn't know I ever go inside the shop."

Ruth laughed.

"Are you sly! It was good of you to trouble, especially on a day like this, but I certainly am pleased. My folks send me such wonderful parcels, I don't like to ask for anything extra. What with packing and postage, those parcels make a hole in their budget. They would never say so, but I know. All the same, I have been thinking of mentioning cereals. Little Paul gets tired of the same breakfast every day, and I think that it is so important for a child to start the day right, don't you? When Paul has eaten a good plate of cereal I know he is going out protected. There are a wonderful lot of vitamins in those foods. But if I feed him on one food too long he gets tired of it and just won't eat it; you know the way children are."

Emma thought of George, Peter and Andrew, at Paul's age, sitting around the table eating large plates of porridge. Neither she nor Dad would have thought it possible they could refuse their porridge unless they were ill. You gave children food and they ate it. Of course some were harder than others to feed, but in the end they ate, or they were punished. However, nobody but a fool would be so tactless as to say those sort of things to a daughter-in-law. She nodded as if in agreement.

"Does Peter eat a cereal? Little boys seem to copy anything their father does." Ruth unconsciously stiffened. Emma noticed this and thought, "Something to do with Paul, I should think." She went on as if she had noticed nothing, "But I suppose Peter insists on porridge?"

Ruth relaxed.

"He surely does. I don't think he thinks it is possible to begin a day any other way. Anyhow, he has gone before I give Paul his breakfast. Peter's always in a rush, and I think it is bad for a child to hurry over his food. Paul sits down just as Peter finishes, and that gives him nice time before we need to start for his school."

"The trouble's not over Paul's food, then," thought Emma. "Perhaps it's to do with his school."

"Does he still like school? He must have been there about six weeks, hasn't he? Has the excitement died down?"

"Why no, he just loves that place. I don't think he learns anything; but, then, at four that's right. I don't think you want to force little children."

"Is he making any friends?"

Ruth saw in her mind the two children who had been to tea yesterday. They had seen the water thrown at Paul; were they repeating the tale at school? Again unconsciously she stiffened. Her voice took on a reserved note which was foreign to her.

"I just wouldn't know about that."

"Sounds rather as if it is Paul's school," thought Emma. "I wonder if it is anything to do with his cousins."

"I suppose he doesn't see much of Geoffrey, Wendy or Jimmie?"

"I guess not. He doesn't say much about them. Geoffrey is way up above him . . ."

"I should hope so," Emma interrupted; "he's seven."

"And Wendy's five and a half, so she is with older children."

"I should think you'll find Paul will soon catch Wendy up; she's slow at her lessons, George thinks. He was the clever one, you know." Emma smiled, aware that she was speaking as she should not and enjoying doing so. She gave a poor imitation of Anna's voice: "I think Wendy must take after my family."

Ruth looked up, her eyes dancing. She had recognised Emma's imitation of Anna. She had never spoken of Anna's voice to anybody, not even to Peter, but she hated it. It was what people at home meant when they said with loathing that somebody spoke with an English accent. She had discovered with surprise that the accent which grated on the American ear was rare in England, in fact Anna was the only person she had met who had it, though she frequently heard it on the radio. But it was news to her that it grated on English people. Yet from Emma's imitation it sounded as though at any rate she found it funny. Between herself and Emma there was friendliness and warmth, though hedged in with a barrier of caution. Ruth the stranger always felt her way in England, and thought before she spoke. She supposed that to her in-laws and their friends in their funny, old-fashioned town she sometimes seemed raw or maybe crude, and that they suspected that inside she criticised many things, which was true; she tried not to, but she did. As her eyes twinkled into Emma's, something new grew between them. It was as if they were spinning a little thread, fine as a spider's, but as strong and as durable. She had the wisdom not to tug at the thread. It was not like Mum-Tring to poke fun at Anna or Doris, and it was best to let the little joke pass.

"I guess, if you are as pretty as little Wendy, there's no need to trouble with school. That child ought to be in pictures."

"I think that's what Anna feels."

"I just can't figure how she can plan to send Geoffrey away to boarding-school next year; I surely would hate that for Paul."

"She'll send Wendy to a boarding-school too, poor mite. Her father's paying, you know. It was marrying beneath her to marry George, and her family feel her children should be educated to her station in life."

This was one of the moments when Ruth felt completely the foreigner. Emma's statement had been calm and unemotional. It made Ruth mad to think anyone could be as silly and snobbish as Anna, or as dumb as Emma to accept such a crazy way of thinking. George, as Emma had said, was the clever one. He had refused to go into Tring's, but had become a solicitor, and was doing very well. What had Anna or her family to get snooty about? Anna's father was only a dentist; what was so splendid about that? With an effort she kept her thoughts to herself.

"Of course Jimmie's only older than Paul by a few months, but I guess Paul will never catch up with that streak of lightning. My, is that boy clever!"

"Doris has decided he's to win every type of scholarship." Without knowing it, a note of pity crept into Emma's voice. "Poor Jimmie! already he's sent to school to work; Doris doesn't approve of even little children playing at lessons. She was brilliant herself, you know. She only went to the ordinary local school, but from there she got a scholarship for a grammar school, and from there one to the London School of Economics, and then she had a wonderful job, I believe."

Ruth did not answer that; she too had done well, she too had left a wonderful job, but it was an accepted thing in the Tring family that it was Doris who was the clever one, and certainly she was clever to talk to. She knew the answers to everything and did not expect to be argued with. Ruth did not approve of a child of not yet five being able to read quite difficult headlines in the newspaper, but there was no doubt about it, Doris's child did make other mothers wonder if they were raising their children right. It was fortunate at the moment there could be no competition between Paul and Jimmie, for naturally Paul was in the lowest grade. She got up and put her empty cup on the tray.

"Well, I surely don't want little Paul to be forced, for he finds school fun, and that's the way it ought to be."

Ruth had spoken more firmly than she knew. Emma looked at her. It was impossible that Peter could want to force Paul; he had never shone at school himself, and had not cared, when school for Paul was first discussed, whether he was sent or not. He had left the decision to

Ruth. All the same, Emma was sure that in some way Paul was the centre of the trouble that she had sensed yesterday. Ruth was inclined to look upon Paul as her property; it could easily be that Peter had interfered in some way; that would account for Ruth not being herself and Peter totally unaware that anything was wrong. Peter, like all the Trings, would order his child about if he thought fit, but having done so would let the matter pass out of his mind. How much tact she had used when her boys were growing up, when she thought it necessary to get her own way without Dad knowing she was getting her own way. She felt for words which would sound natural but which would hint at this.

"They're a funny lot, the Trings. Talking of Jimmie working, and you not wanting Paul forced, puts me in mind of when my boys were growing up. Dad, you know, and his sisters went to the local school, as their father had done. Dad reckoned in their line of business they had to be able to read, write and do arithmetic, but nothing in the way of what he calls 'fancy education'. He believed that the great thing was to put a boy into his business young. Then, of course, George got that scholarship for the grammar school. Dad didn't want him to take it at first, said he'd get above himself and think himself too good for the shop. Well, dear, you must have found out a long time ago that you can't force a Tring, but you can work them round to thinking something is their own idea. That's what I did: I kept working at Dad until one day I heard him say to one of his old customers in ever so proud a voice, 'My boy George is going to the grammar school. I've got three boys, so two will be enough for the shop. I reckon George will do something different; he's got brains.'"

"It was wonderfully fortunate that Peter and Andrew did not win scholarships."

"Peter never would have, you know that, dear. He never was a boy for his books; but Andrew might have, only the war came and Peter was called up, so Andrew left school at fourteen to help his Dad." Emma gave a chuckle. "The funny thing was, George having got his scholarship and Dad having agreed that he should take it, Dad came to think it had been his idea that the other boys should have scholarships too. Then I had to work on Dad again. I had to make him think he hadn't wanted Peter to have a scholarship. I made him see about Peter at the time, but if you ask Dad now he'll tell you he always meant both boys to have a posh education the same as George had done, only Peter hadn't the brains and the war spoiled Andrew's chance."

"Was Andrew sour because he had to miss that good education?"

Emma sighed.

"To tell the you truth, dear, I've never been quite happy about Andrew; you see, he would have had a scholarship if it hadn't been for Peter being called up. He's clever, you know—thinks a lot and goes to lectures. It was at something called a summer school, whatever that may be, that he met Doris. It was to do with politics, I think, for some day he'll be standing for the Council and all that, same as Dad did." She lowered her voice. "But what I'm afraid of is that, with Doris to push him, he'll have different politics. Of course it's never spoken of, but I believe she's Labour. There'll be a lot of trouble with Dad if that crops up; the

Trings have always been Conservative, and they'd lose a lot of custom if that was to happen. Still, I shall manage; I won't stand for quarrels; there is enough in the world as it is, I say, so let's keep them out of the family." Emma had, she thought, dropped her hint about the Trings into Ruth's ear. She got up and kissed her. "Well, I must be going; I interrupted you writing a letter, and it will soon be time for you to fetch Paul from school."

Anna and Doris, with their babies in their perambulators, were standing outside the school. They had nothing in common, but were drawn together as two seasick passengers might be drawn together, by mutual suffering. Both girls felt they had made sacrifices in marrying their husbands, and both felt their sacrifices were unappreciated, not only by their husbands, but by the family of their husbands.

Anna knew she could have endured her lowered status if only the Trings, and that included George, said such things as "I know it's not what you've been used to" or "It's wonderful the way you manage seeing the way you were brought up." But the Trings not only never said such things but clearly never thought them. They—and again this maddeningly included George—seemed to think she was a lucky girl to have a husband who was doing well and therefore could afford to pay someone to come and help in the house. There was George, and her three children; she had everything any woman could ask for. What no Tring understood was that, with a name like theirs, the people she and George knew were of the tradesmen world. The wives of the clergy, doctors, dentists, solicitors and other professional people who would have been in her set had she been at home seemed scarcely to know that she existed, nor—which she minded more—that her children existed. She found this ignoring of her children hard to bear, for she took an infinity of trouble to see they crossed the paths of children of the type she thought they should know. She took both Geoffrey and Wendy to the right dancing class, and the right gymnasium class, and while they were there never missed an opportunity of mentioning that her father practised in Harley Street, and that though the little school that the children attended was all right for now, it would not do when they were older. It was best to send children to boarding-schools, for it was so difficult to regulate who they knew if they were educated in their home town. The various mothers she sought out for these confidences smiled and said how right she was, and how lovely little Wendy looked, and wasn't Geoffrey growing into a fine boy. Having spoken they would move away and talk to their own friends, amongst whom (which Anna was spared from knowing) she was called Mrs. "Jist-Fency" Tring.

Doris was dissatisfied with Andrew for different reasons. Hers was a mind that believed it knew all the answers. Mentally she sliced people up as if they were cake, and dropped the slices into appropriately labelled boxes. Slices of Mum and Dad-Tring lived in boxes marked "Reactionaries", "Self-satisfied middle-classes" and "Mental inertia". That there was no need for her to tie the pair together as if they were Tweedledee and Tweedledum did not cross her mind. One of the things Doris knew beyond argument was that reactionary women of the lower middle-classes never thought for themselves, but followed their husbands in everything. Knowing this, that, as far as Mum and Dad-Tring was concerned, was that. She sliced children up in exactly the same way. Such phrases as "Children like this . . ."or "Children can understand that . . ." were constantly on her lips. She disbelieved what some fools said that what was suitable for one child at five another child might not be ready for till it was ten. She knew it was all in the way you brought children up. She admitted to herself that when she first met Andrew, or rather when she had known Andrew for a short while, she had put several slices of him into the totally wrong boxes. But this had not shaken her belief that her understanding of human beings was infallible. At the summer school, when she had first met Andrew, she was satisfied she had sliced him correctly. Pieces of him had dropped very properly into boxes marked "Son of reactionary parents", "Needs help to free himself from smugness and middle-class satisfaction", "Good brain if freed from effects of clogging upbringing". But as the days passed she discovered that even a clear-thinking, ambitious girl like herself could fall in love as completely as a brainless, pretty-pretty fool. It was at that time that her vision, obscured by Andrew's good looks, caused her to toss great slices of Andrew into boxes where they could not possibly belong. "Fine brain", "Natural leader", "With suitable wife could get anywhere", "Brilliant speaker", "Should consider Parliament". It was quite a time after she and Andrew were married before she accepted how wrong her late slicings had been. Briskly—for self-pity was not a failing of hers—she picked the slices out of the wrong boxes and dropped them into new ones. She left the first slices undisturbed, except to nod at their boxes to say "How right I was, how ghastly right!" "Son of reactionary parents, God, how true!" "Needs help to free himself. How he needs help! But will he ever be freed?" But the slice in the box marked "Fine brain" she moved into a box marked "Mediocre thinker". "Natural leader" slipped easily into a box with the label "Could be big fish if pond small enough". She had no place except a dustbin box for the slice labelled "With suitable wife could get anywhere", and into this too went "Should consider Parliament". "Brilliant speaker" she put into a box which she kept constantly under her eye, for it was labelled "Write Andrew's speeches for him or will talk reactionary drivel". All the same, though she was dissatisfied with her re-sliced Andrew, passion, and with it love of a kind for him, remained. It was not the love Doris wanted to give, and thought she was born to give, a love based on mutual respect and understanding; rather it was exasperated love, such as a mother might bestow on an unsatisfactory but still cherished child.

Anna and Doris, for lack of another subject, discussed their babies. Anna's Caroline, a delicious sight, under a pink rug with a rabbit appliqued on the corner, dimpling and smiling at a cosy, but unhygienic, once-white fur dog. Doris's John, his face red and shining from ceaseless contact with the weather, propped sensibly upright against a hard macintosh pillow, his small body buried under a green macintosh coverlet, smiling and dimpling at a washable, and therefore hygienic, plastic dog. As Ruth appeared on the horizon they broke off their conversation. Ruth was cement to their uneasy friendship; it was not that they disliked her as an individual, but they disliked the approval that was showered on her, and especially they disliked her apparently completely uncritical satisfaction with the place and people with whom her lot was cast, and especially her satisfaction with Mum and Dad-Tring. "If it were not impossible," Doris frequently said to Anna, "you would almost think Ruth admired Mum-Tring," to which Anna usually replied, "Sucking up." The fact that she pronounced sucking as sicking made this supposed behaviour on the part of Ruth sound particularly revolting. Further cement to their friendship was the fact that Ruth had only one child, and though Anna worshipped her three and Doris—though she hid it well—her two, it did not prevent both girls from feeling it was unjust that they should be tied to nappy-washing and perambulators while Ruth, free as a summer breeze, could spend the whole day on her home. No wonder Mum and Dad-Tring and their friends were always singing Ruth's praises as a housewife; anybody, as they frequently pointed out to each other, could be a perfect housewife if they had the whole day to spend on being one. That Ruth longed for another baby could not prevent them from feeling aggravated when they considered her freedom from babies.

This morning Ruth's babyless condition appeared unusually annoying. The damp cold, when movements were slowed down by a perambulator, made faces both look and feel blue and striped. Ruth, marching gaily down the road, her cheeks pink and glowing, unencumbered by anything save a small handbag and an umbrella, looked aggravatingly like a magazine-cover girl.

In the school cloakroom the children were dressing themselves to go home. Anna's Geoffrey had reached the stage when he needed to be under a schoolmaster. He was a big boy for his age, and had to display his masculinity and dislike of feminine dominance by shouting and knocking other boys about. He was not a bully at heart, but tears and squeals at his approach made him feel a man. Dressed for home in his blue overcoat, his school cap pulled over one eye, he was enjoying himself jeering at his cousin Paul.

Wendy was exquisite and knew it. A fair-haired, blue-eyed, daintily dressed dream of what a little girl should look like. Wendy had not waited to be out of nappies before she had got on to her charms. Cooing in her pram, she became accustomed to murmurs of admiration. One smile she discovered, and she could have anything she wanted. By the time she could toddle she had learnt what she could do with her eyes. At four, much encouraged by her parents, she behaved like a professional beauty. Going to school merely added to her admirers. Even had the school not accepted immediately that she was a darling and a beauty, Wendy would not have noticed it, for her belief in her charms gave her such poise and assurance that glances and words that were not full of admiration slid off her. Now, looking a little picture, in sky-blue coat, bonnet and leggings, she watched Paul struggling to button his coat. From her expression her thoughts might have been soaring amongst the angels; actually she was enjoying hearing Paul taunted by Geoffrey and the other big boys, conscious that her presence stirred them on.

Doris did not believe in old-fashioned nonsense such as "little pitchers have long ears"; she knew that as soon as possible a child should take its place as a member of the community. A sheltered background in which words were chosen for young ears was of no use to a future world citizen. In spite of Andrew's frowns and nods to remind her of their son's presence, Doris did not change her conversation one iota because Jimmie was in the room. With his first rusks he had sucked in his mother's pitying attitude to his paternal grandparents. He learnt, as surely as he learnt that clocks told the time, that his cousin Paul was spoilt, and likely to be ruined by it, and that anyone who could do anything to toughen him would be doing both Paul and the nation a service. Jimmie did not wear leggings; Doris knew they were not hygienic; he sat on the floor to put on his shoes and, when he could make himself heard, joined in the baiting of Paul. Actually he liked Paul and, on the few occasions when the two little boys were alone, they played together in complete contentment. But it was grand for somebody not yet five to shout with the big boys; besides, it was good for Paul; his mother had said so.

At home Paul could put on his own clothes, though, to save time, Ruth usually helped him. In his first weeks at school the mistresses had praised him for being so capable; there were other children of his age who could scarcely button their coats. The first weeks at school had been fun, and Paul was too small to know what had gone wrong. He knew at home he was very precious, the most important person in the house. He knew Mum thought he was clever and said funny things. He knew his illnesses and upsets mattered to her terribly. In his little mind that was how things would be wherever he was: he would always come first with everybody. Then one day in his class he had a success acting in a song as a cat; pleased with himself, he later gave his cat impersonation in the cloakroom before the school. "Feeble," shouted a voice; another yelled, "What's he trying to be? A cow?" His cousin Geoffrey led the roars of derision. In a moment, Paul's own form, who, so short a while before, had been so admiring, joined in the fun. "Feeble, feeble!" "Silly show-off!" For a moment Paul was too shocked to do anything but stare around with startled eyes, then he lost his temper. He lay on the floor. He kicked. He screamed. In a second a mistress had picked him up and dusted him down, but that had not meant that she sympathised, as his mother would have done. Instead she had said briskly, "Don't behave like a baby, Paul. We'll have to put you in a perambulator." From that day Paul-baiting became a recognised school sport. It did not occur every day, but Paul lived in terror that it would. At any moment Geoffrey's voice might howl, "There's Pauly Pauly perambulator," and "Pauly Pauly perambulator" was screamed round the playground. Without knowing why, in his own form, with children of his own age, Paul became the braggart. When he was a centre of what was going on with all eyes on him he was exhilarated; his cheeks flamed, his eyes shone, the greater the interest he aroused the greater lengths to which he would go. The fear he had of a water-cistern in his home which sometimes gurgled and puffed as if it were alive was the same fear he had for the big boys. For days the water-cistern was a water-cistern, as for days his cousin Geoffrey and the other big boys were ordinary schoolboys. Then suddenly, just as the water-cistern would come alive and gurgle and puff, so the big boys would scream and howl and turn into demons. He was too small to reason that he should keep out of the way of the big boys as much as possible, but just as at home he squeezed past the cistern trying to avoid its notice, so at school, out of his form, he tried to make himself as small and unnoticeable as possible. To-day smallness and inconspicuousness had not helped him; the friends who had been to tea on Sunday had reported that his father had thrown water over him. "Pauly Pauly perambulator," yelled Geoffrey. "Whose father threw water over him?" screamed another child. "He's a fish, that's what he is," yowled a third. Grinning, the school took up the cry: "Pauly Pauly perambulator's a fish. Pauly Pauly perambulator's a fish."

Outside there was excitement amongst the mothers. A van had driven up, and out of it had jumped three men and two cameras. While the camera-men set up their cameras, the third man spoke to the waiting mothers; they were looking for a location to shoot some scenes in a forthcoming film in which a school would be needed; would the mothers mind moving back a little so that the cameras could get a clear shot of the children leaving the school? They hoped to get a spot of sun in a few minutes and shoot a few feet of film before the children realised what was happening.

The mothers were enchanted; they forgot that it was cold; they drew back in an excited, chattering group, each one praying inwardly that her child was looking its engaging best.

Any hopes the film unit had of keeping their presence a secret died the moment Geoffrey and the older boys rushed out of the school. With screams of excitement and cascades of questions they crowded round the nearest camera. The other camera-man moved closer to the school door. As he reached it the sun came out and

Paul, Jimmie and Wendy came down the steps. The sun shone on Wendy's hair as she smiled and waved to her mother. The camera-man went on with his job, but his photographic mind had registered that scene. When he had shot what he wanted he joined his two companions.

"There was a kid I photographed . . ." He looked round; no mother or child had, of course, left. "It's that little fair girl holding on to that pram; 'course the light's lousy, so you can't tell, but I'd say it was worth taking the mother's name and address."

It was no surprise to anyone Wendy being noticed; it was so certain that if anyone was it would be Wendy that there was not even much jealousy. The mothers crowded round Anna.

"What did he say?"

"Did he want to film her by herself?"

"I always said she ought to be in pictures."

Anna glowed inwardly, though seeming outwardly composed. The man had just asked for Wendy's name and address. He had said it was only a chance, but it might be his company would want to see her and make a test. Anna felt sure it was not just a chance; she was convinced that a picture of Wendy had only to lie before an experienced eye and the child would at once be given a film contract and become a star.

The mothers dispersed homewards saddened. How wonderful to be Mrs. George Tring! Anna knew what they were thinking, and her heart sang. At last it was going to be wonderful to be Mrs. George Tring. With Wendy in pictures she could snap her fingers at the dancing and gymnasium class children. Then the parents of those children would come sucking up to her; but let them suck.

They had up till now taken her at George's standard, though they could see she came out of a totally different box; now she would treat them as the smalltown people that they were.

Ruth let Paul wait, and the cameras were back in their van and the van driven away before she turned towards home. Paul, excited by the film unit, had forgotten the scene in the cloakroom; he danced beside Ruth pouring out questions.

"How did that wheel-thing the man turned make a photograph, Mum?" "How did a photograph come inside the camera, Mum?" "Is the man paid to take photographs, Mum, or does he do it for fun?"

Ruth laughed.

"I'm sorry, honey, but I just don't know one thing about it. But we'll be able to find out for you. One of those men told Aunty Anna that they could maybe use little Wendy in a movie."

Paul threw up his head.

"I'll be in a movie too." He pulled his hand from his mother's and threw himself about. "This is me acting in a movie. Look, Mum, look at me."

Ruth looked and her heart ached; this was the side of Paul that worried her. He was behaving not as an ordinary small boy but as an exhibitionist small boy. She wished she knew how to treat him. What made him have to act in this crazy fashion? Ruth never raised her voice or spoke severely to Paul; she was sure that was the wrong way to handle a child.

"I have looked, dear. Now come back to me. Paul! Paul dear! Mum is calling you."

Paul in his prancings was obliterating "Pauly Pauly perambulator". Ruth had to call him three times before he heard her, and then, though he held her hand and stopped his prancings, it was quite a while before he quietened. She looked down at his head, and love and anxiety tugged at her heart. He was so little, so in need of protection; if only she knew what was making him act so strangely. It was something to do with his school, she was sure of that; he had always been inclined to be a little naughty if he did not get his own way, but that was only natural; she was sure she had been naughty herself if she did not get her own way when she was a child. It was these last weeks that his naughty turns had become worse, especially this showing off and talking in a loud, silly way. If only he was not so small! Why, he was only a baby—far too small for questioning to do any good.

They passed a bookshop. Without planning to do so, Ruth stopped; almost as if her feet were leading her she went in. The assistant asked what she wanted. Ruth looked at his fair, young, vague face and, first directing Paul to a shelf of children's books, replied with caution:

"Some book on children's neuroses." The assistant gazed at her blankly. "Dumb cluck," she thought, "he won't know the first thing I'm talking about." Almost she left the shop, but her need for help made her struggle on. She spoke to the assistant in the gentle, slow way she talked to Paul, "Maybe you have some place where you display educational and medical books."

In a dark corner there were two shelves of such books. At first it seemed to Ruth there was nothing to help or interest her; her eyes wandered over titles to do with schools, parenthood and how to bring up baby. Suddenly she pulled out a large book in a grey cover, *The Mind and the Child*. Inside she read the words "Mental Hygiene". She opened the book at random. "The child", she read, "is dependent on his parents, but he must be recognised as an individual with his own tastes and talents, and must not be forced into a mould chosen by the parents. Forcing a child into a mould which it does not fit may start a mental illness. As an example a child with strong individuality compressed into too small a mould may be forced to thrash out in order to make room for his ego. This thrashing out, if misunderstood, may cause great distress to the parents and harm to the child. It may take the form of exhibitionism, and in extreme cases lead to such symptoms as stealing . . ." Ruth looked anxiously round for Paul. He was sitting on the floor happily study-ing the latest adventures of Orlando the Marmalade Cat. Too carried away by what she had just read to accept the fact that as far as she knew he had never had an inclination to steal anything, she sighed with relief that Orlando was too big a book for him to conceal as he left the shop. She returned to *The Mind and the Child*, she turned over several pages, with widening eyes as terrify-ing words danced before them—"schizophrenic, neurotic depression, paranoiac, neurotic compulsion, kleptomania, neurotic alcoholism"—she closed the book. How frighten-ing! All these just from wrong upbringing—from crushing little Paul's individuality, from fitting him into the Tring mould, killing his taste and talent. This wise book said that exhibitionism was one of the signs of a compressed child. Hadn't she been worrying about that very thing? Paul's need to be the centre of every picture, his naughty turns, to-day's silly showing off about the movies. When you read a book like this, how clear everything became! Of course he had to pretend it was he who was in a movie; that was just giving his ego room. To admit that Wendy was smarter than he was made him mentally ill. He was thrashing out, breaking up the Tring mould. She beckoned to the salesman.

"This is just what I wanted. I will take it."

The news about Wendy, in garbled form, took no time to reach Tring's. Mothers often popped into Tring's for something as they took the children home from school, and to-day there was no need to buy anything; what they had to tell was so exciting old Mr. Tring or his sons would think their time well spent just hearing it. This was not Dad-Tring's point of view. Towards twelve-thirty, when things quietened down, he came across to Peter and Andrew.

"I suppose you've had those cackling women at you, too? Putting ideas into poor Anna's head, as if it wasn't full enough of silliness as it is."

Andrew and Peter were checking packages for a special delivery. Peter grinned at his father.

"You'd think Wendy was a star already from the way they talk."

Andrew took the matter more seriously.

"I hope nothing comes of it; she's a pretty little thing, I've no doubt of that."

Peter checked the last package.

"That's the lot. What can come of it? George wouldn't allow it."

Andrew shook his head. Peter was the lucky one; he had not got an ambitious wife.

"I wouldn't be too sure; it'll please Anna."

Dad-Tring, standing squarely in his shop, his hands thrust deeply into his apron pockets, his face almost as weather-beaten and tough-looking as the cliffs of Dover, laughed out loud.

"Never heard such nonsense. Anna's a silly little thing, and I daresay can twist George a bit, but she can't twist him that far. Actin'! In pictures! A baby no more than five years old! Disgustin'!"

Peter laid the packages in a box.

"Too right, Dad. If Ruth came to me with nonsense of that sort—which she never would—I'd soon put it out of her head."

Andrew looked wearily at his brother. Make—make—make. Dad and Peter were slick with that word, but he'd like to see either of them make Doris do something she hadn't a mind to, and he knew George felt the same about Anna.

"How'd you make her?"

Peter thought contentedly about last night. He never spoke of his deep love for Ruth, and torture could not have dragged a word out of him about the physical side of their love. Inwardly he smiled as he remembered how Ruth had tried to talk some nonsense about Paul when they were in bed, and how he had stopped her.

"I'd buy her a new hat. Isn't that right, Dad?"

"That's the ticket, son; nothing takes a woman's mind off a thing like a new hat."

Andrew untied his apron. He spoke sharply. "I'm going out for my dinner."

It was the Tring custom to lunch behind the shop. A woman cooked it for the three men, and beer was brought over daily from "The Green Man" opposite. Dad-Tring raised surprised, enquiring eyebrows at Andrew's departing back.

"What's up with him? Doris playing up?"

Peter disliked discussing his brother's affairs, but Doris's cleverness and her ambition to pull Andrew up to her standard were common knowledge.

"Spent his Sunday having his head stuffed with a lot of highbrow nonsense, shouldn't wonder."

Dad-Tring shouted at his two girl employees to warn them that he and Mr. Peter were going to eat.

"Lot of damn foolishness; if I had that young woman alone for half an hour I'd take a slipper to her; that would be the end of all this educational foolery." He jerked his head sideways in a friendly way to Peter. "You knew a thing or two, young feller-me-lad, when you picked your Ruthie. Now, there's a wife in a hundred: cooks well, keeps your home well, looks nice and doesn't want to do the thinking."

Peter smiled happily.

"That's right, Dad. I'm lucky and I know it."

CHAPTER 2
THE MIST GATHERS

RUTH's heart was warmed as it was warmed each year by the beauty of the spring. The gardens that she passed as she took Paul to and from school were so gay with spring bulbs and blossom, and the lilac-buds were swelling; her heart always lifted at lilac time. Something—the spring, perhaps—was pumping hope and courage into her veins; she was worrying less, maybe because it was almost Easter—the festival of faith. She knew everything was going to turn out right; she would be guided to find a way to handle the problem of Paul without upsetting Peter. She had read *The Mind and the Child* through twice, and special portions of it several times. It was wonderful the help it gave. She almost felt as if she knew the author; he was an old friend with whom she could sit down and talk over her worries. On his advice she had bought an exercise-book and written down his questions about Paul, and her answers. When had she first seen signs of mental disturbance, the author asked her? That had been an easy one. Right from the beginning. The first time, as far as she could remember, was an occasion when she had first tried to cure him of throwing his toys out of his perambulator. She had given him an old toy dog which was finished with, so when he threw it out of his perambulator she could leave it lying in the street. Poor little soul! she had not realised how fond he was of that dog. He had screamed terribly. She had thought he would have a fit.

Even after she had run back and fetched the dog and cuddled him and given him candy it had taken quite a while to calm him down. She wished she could ask her friend, the author, just what that signified. Could it be seeing his dog lying on the pavement showed that he felt he was missing affection, and, instead of picking the old dog up, she should have gone off right away and bought him a new and better dog? But the book had not mentioned throwing toys out of perambulators, so she just had to write the answer down and leave it at that. Reading back her answers to the author's questions,

Ruth realised that by putting things down she was learning a lot. She saw that right up to the time he went to school all Paul's naughty fits had been connected with herself. The answer to that was, she gathered, "stealing mother-love" or maybe "neurotic infantilism". Reading through her answers she could see it was going to school that had made him worse. Have the attacks increased recently? Sure they had, right since Christmas there had been almost daily screaming fits, holding of breath and showing off. Was there an increase of symptoms while the child was away from home? Why no, the school said he was a lovely little boy, no trouble to anyone. Yet being sent to school had aggravated his trouble. This, the author said, meant that the danger of neurotic infantilism was aggravated by separation from the mother. Could it be, Ruth wondered, but unfortunately could not get hold of the author to ask him, that it was equally caused, or possibly entirely caused, by Peter's intention that Paul should grow up a typical Tring?

It was the last day of school term and, though nobody knew it except herself, an important day for Ruth. Tomorrow, when the holidays started, was the day when, guided by her friend, the author of *The Mind and the Child*, she would start her plan for freeing Paul's ego. The author said that in cases where there were marked symptoms of neurotic infantilism it would be well to take the advice of a trained psychiatrist. The author made it clear that he was layman writing for laymen, but where treatment was required, a layman wouldn't do; it must be a mental doctor. But Ruth knew no mental doctors. She had heard they were attached to all big hospitals and there were guidance clinics for children, but to get Paul accepted as a patient in a big London hospital, with constant attendance at a guidance clinic, meant their own doctor would have to be called and persuaded that the treatment was needed, and Peter would have to know about it. Their own doctor, though Ruth was sure he was a well-meaning man and did his best with the gifts he had, never had inspired confidence in her. He was the kind of doctor that the British, especially the Tring sort of British, trusted—mostly, she was inclined to think, because he was the vicar's warden at the church and the leading comedian in the Amateur Dramatic Society. No matter how much anxiety there was, he would come into the house and right away tell Peter a funny story in a whisper, or call out, "Well, Mrs. Peter, is he dying again? You know, if your boy was really ill I believe you'd buy a wreath before I could get here." Ruth felt that kind of conversation in bad taste. It was right and natural a mother should be anxious when her little son was ill or, if it came to that, if she or Peter were ill. Illness was something that should be treated gravely; it was never a matter for laughter. As for telling Peter that she wanted Paul to attend a child's guidance clinic, it was just not to be thought of. He would either howl with laughter or he could be annoyed, as now and again he was annoyed when she talked of things he could not understand. She wished that the author of *The Mind and the Child* lived in England. If he had she would have written to him and asked if he thought her plan for Paul was a good one, explaining at the same time the difficulties in the way of taking him to a psychiatrist; but she gathered from the introduction to the book that her friend, the author, lived in America, and it seemed too difficult to carry on an intimate correspondence at that distance. The author was fond of the words "compensate" and "compensatory". Ruth gathered this meant that if a child felt he was being torn too soon from the protection of his mother he must be compensated in some way. If he did not get extra attention and admiration in some other way he might become a divided personality. Her friend, the author, explained a divided personality in a very simple way. He wrote it was as if there were a quarrel in a family, and as a result one half of the home was divided against the other half. If a child felt a need of approval and admiration, it was the same need that he felt for food. A hungry child would find food somehow, and a child hungry for approval and admiration would find those somehow. Since she had studied *The Mind and the Child* more and more clearly Ruth saw in Paul how true all this was. Wasn't Paul's screaming, holding his breath and behaving in a silly and affected way just to hold attention? This holiday she must get him snapped right out of his trouble; he must be compensated for his feeling of being torn away from her before he got bogged down and it was too late to do anything. If only he were a girl! The book said that new frocks and a pretty string of beads had made all the difference to a little girl of the author's acquaintance. The author knew several boys whose mental stability had been helped, but none of the things which had helped them seemed right for Paul. The author knew a boy whose whole mental outlook had changed because Dad and Mum had taken his playing in the junior baseball team seriously. He said that once they made a feature of his baseball in the home, the child had got straightened out, and had never looked back. But Paul was too small for sports. At one moment, Ruth had thought horse-back riding might help. She had seen two small children out riding, looking smart and pretty, and had pointed them out to Paul.

"Would you like to learn horse-back riding, Paul?"

Paul had shrunk against her.

"Horses bite."

Ruth remembered a horse belonging to the milkman who had frightened Paul by nuzzling at his ear.

"No, dear, that horse did not bite. It was kissing you. Mum explained that to you right away."

Paul had said no more about the horse biting, but neither had he agreed that it had kissed him, so Ruth gave up the idea of horse-riding lessons. The book said that a child in Paul's mental condition should not be forced to take part in any sport at which he did not excel. All the same, the horse idea had been a help; it had pushed her into giving up looking at sports or anything of that sort to compensate him, and instead had turned her to his daily life. That was when, almost as if the author were whispering in her ear, she had seen what she should do. That was why this last day of the term was so important: this was the day when the compensating was to begin. Soon after they left the house on their way to school Ruth took a deep breath so that she did not speak in a rush, but chose her words carefully:

"Mum is so proud to-day."

Paul hopped on one leg.

"Can you hop, Mum? I bet you can't hop as long on one leg as me."

"Mum was speaking to you, dear. She was telling you she was so proud to-day. Do you know why?"

"I hopped twenty times on one leg; Wendy said I didn't, but I did."

"Stop hopping, Paul, and attend to Mum. Do you know why Mum's proud to-day?" She felt that Paul was not going to answer, so regretfully, because she had planned he would give her a cue for the next part of her speech, she went on, "Mum is proud because to-morrow you start your Easter holidays. I guess you can't figure how proud a mother is when she has a boy big enough to have holidays."

Paul hopped on the other foot.

"Is it only me who has holidays, or do the others have them too?"

"They all have holidays; but a boy's first holidays are something very precious and important, and I am planning just lovely things that you and I will do. We're going to have the best time."

Paul continued to hop.

"I'll buy a water-pistol like Geoffrey has, and I'll hide round corners, and every time anybody from school comes by I'll bounce out and shoot at them, and they'll be so frightened that they'll fall down dead."

Ruth wished that the author of *The Mind and the Child* could have heard that. How right he was! That was the kind of dangerous tendency of which he had warned her.

"Now, Paul, that's not a nice way to talk. When you go to bed you must ask God to forgive you for saying a thing like that."

Paul stumbled, and had to skip to catch up with her.

"I'll say 'Matthew, Mark, Luke and John, Bless the bed that I lie on, And four good angels guard my bed, Two at the foot and two at the head,' but none of them won't mind about the water-pistol. I see those four angels: the two at the top watching the door with their little beady eyes to see no one comes in; the two at the bottom wait for burglars, and they've got water-pistols just like Geoffrey's, only much, much bigger."

Ruth, after a pause to show disapproval at this foolish talk, went back to her theme.

"Because you are a big boy who has a holiday, Mum is wondering what you'd like to do to-morrow. She thought it would be fun to take a bag of bread and go to the park to feed the ducks; what does Paul think?"

The park was some distance away, and Paul had not visited it for nearly a year. He frowned, trying to remember what ducks looked like.

"Was they dressed as sailors?"

"Who, dear?"

"Ducks." Paul frowned more than ever, trying to see the pond and the ducks. "Was they wearing little hats?"

For one moment Ruth was puzzled, then she laughed.

"No, darling! that's Donald Duck. He's only on the movies; the park ducks are real ducks. Then do you know what I thought? You would go round the little pond in one of those miniature boats; you remember riding in a boat last year, don't you?"

Last year was aeons away, and Paul could neither recall nor was interested in what he had done when he was three. Instead, finding his mother in so exceptionally giving a mood, he rubbed his face against her coat.

"For my holiday could we have a el-fant to stay with us?"

Ruth saw that he was thinking of Babar. *The Mind and the Child* had not been explicit on ages; it had not mentioned how old a child should be before you started to teach it. Maybe it was no good talking to someone as small as Paul; he should just be made to feel how important his holidays were to her, and see what lovely treats she planned for him.

"I think our house'd be a little small for an elephant, don't you? But we'll fix some lovely treats. Mum wants you to have a wonderful time. She is so very, very proud of her big son."

Paul looked up at her puzzled.

"Am I big? At school I'm one of the littlest."

Ruth did not answer; instead she looked up at the clear blue spring sky. She must not be discouraged. It was spring-time—the time of faith. Paul was very small. But in spite of her brave thoughts, some of the spring-time joy ran out of the day. That word "littlest". There was quite a piece about that in the book—something to do with the severing of the natal cord. It seemed there were children who refused to grow up, who wanted to remain near their mothers, who tried to stay babies so as to hold on to the security of the womb. Maybe this plan for making Paul feel his holidays were important and precious was not so hot, after all. Maybe to keep on using the word "big" was harmful. Oh dear, if only the author of *The Mind and the Child* did not live in America!

Anna was dressing Caroline with one hand and buttoning Wendy with the other when George came into the nursery. She lifted her cheek towards him for his customary farewell morning peck.

"Good-bye, dear. Stand still, Wendy sweetheart, so Mummie can button you." She looked up at George. He had not given her his peck; he was, in fact, just standing doing nothing—a most unusual occurrence. He was always in a rush in the morning. "What is it, George?"

"I'm tired. We'll go away for Easter."

Anna was so certain that a letter about Wendy was coming, even if it was delayed, that she gaped at him.

"We can't. You know we can't go away now."

It had taken George much thought to plan this holiday. The six war years spent overseas, uncomfortable though they were, had been happy. He'd enjoyed the inevitability of everything; he found there always being a superior to direct his fortunes relaxing. Almost it had been a return to childhood. As an officer, he had responsibilities, but they were limited, and not so great as his responsibilities had been at school. He had enjoyed the clubman's life, the Army jokes and the good humour. It was these things that had fooled him into thinking he would like to live permanently in the world from which many of his brother officers sprang. That was why one leave he had married Anna.

George's was a contented spirit; it had taken him a long while to admit to himself that he detested the life he now led. There had been no chance during the war to see the shape his life with Anna might take. He had little imagination, so he could not invent a shape he could not see. After he was married, when his leave was up, he had rejoined his regiment, and Anna had gone back to her job in the War Office. When peace was declared he had thought it wonderfully lucky that a house belonging to his father had become vacant and he, Anna and baby Geoffrey could start life in his home town. It was slow dripping, as of water on a stone, that had worn away his contentment. He had not realised for quite a time that, whatever he might plan, Anna was determined to change him and make a gentleman of him. At first he accepted with smiling good-humour a row of petty rules: never wash your hands in the kitchen—say "pardon" when hiccups or other noises escape you—George dear, don't help yourself to butter with your knife, there is a butter-knife; a mass of silly little points which added together amounted to nothing, but each in itself when repeated caused as much irritability as constant rubbing at a gnat bite. When Anna said "George", in her over-refined way, George found himself wanting to do something really common, such as spitting or putting out his tongue. His childhood had been happy; his mother was a real homemaker, and his home was a jolly place full of warmth and cosiness, lacking in fuss. His father, though a bit of a disciplinarian, had been a companion to his boys, and had taken an interest in all they did. George, in his easy-going way, had taken it for granted that his and Anna's home would be more or less a replica of his parents' home. He could not put his finger on where it differed, but on one occasion when Anna had reproved him for some solecism he had found himself muttering, "Lot of damned whimsy-whamsy", and knew he had described satisfactorily his whole life. Anna was whimsy-whamsy about the children. Geoffrey was all right—a nice, manly little chap—but what did Anna want to drag the poor kid to dancing classes for? Enough to turn him into a sissy. Naturally he hated it; what boy wouldn't? George did not hold with boarding-schools, no Tring did; he would have insisted that Geoffrey had tried for a scholarship at his old day school, but he had given in for Geoffrey's sake. It had got his goat to hear the endless stream of advice poured on the poor child. "Not like that, dear; a gentleman never . . ." George reckoned that when Geoffrey got to the boarding-school he would have the surprise of his life when he discovered how many of the things he had learnt gentlemen never did, young gentlemen who went to boarding-school did every day. He had not broken the news to Anna, but Wendy was not going to a boarding-school. She was the pride of his life, and he was not going to put up with having her packed away where he could not see her for most of the year. To hell with her making nice friends! Nice friends be damned! He wanted his little girl to make friends with the local children and marry one of the local boys some day, and live in the town, where as a family they were known and respected; to hell with this film nonsense! Thank goodness nothing had come of it. If Anna thought he was going to let his little girl be poodle-faked around, stared at by every Tom, Dick and Harry, she had another thought coming. He was miserably conscious that partly because of his job, but mostly because of Anna, he was adrift; he was the queer Tring who belonged nowhere. He had lost the solid Tring world, and in exchange he had got Anna's whimsy-whamsy world. He had scarcely a friend that Anna approved of and neither had his children, and though the children had come to no harm so far, they were being brought up chockful of snobbish nonsense, which could do them no good in the long run.

It was brooding on these things, or perhaps the feeling of spring in the air, which had made George decide he must have a break. As usual, having no imagination, he did not see Anna and the children having the break, but merely the sort of break that he thought they ought to enjoy. They would go to a farm in Devonshire or Cornwall—some place miles from anywhere—with nothing to look at but the countryside and the animals; the kids could run wild, he might do a bit of fishing, and perhaps in the changed atmosphere have a talk with Anna and see if they could re-plan their home life on a better footing. Anyway, whether he had that talk with Anna or not, the break would do the girl a lot of good, do them all a lot of good. Carried away at the thought of open spaces, he had sung a line or two of "Devon—glorious Devon." The farm—he couldn't exactly visualise the farm, except that there would be masses of food heaped on to plates, a smell of sweat, broad conversation about farm doings, in which manure was called manure and animals who gave birth gave birth, and there were no polite coughs and talk about "little strangers". A good, tough, he-man, weatherbeaten sort of life where nobody cared what you did or said, what implements you ate with, whether your hands were washed, or what you wore. He had prepared for a certain amount of argument on Anna's part, but he was determined that he would take his family to a farm, and for once was going to wear the trousers and make her do what he wanted. The dogged Tring strain in him had weakened, but there was still enough of it for him to pull on when needed.

"Of course we can go; do you a world of good."

Anna tried to be patient.

"This film, dear; you know we must be here when the letter comes. Now you must hurry, or you will be late for the office."

George put on his hat at a rakish angle and gave it a tug.

"Film! A lot of nonsense! We'll never hear another word about it, and a good job too."

Anna gave a little scream.

"George! Your hat! How often do I have to remind you a gentleman never wears a hat in the house?" She pulled Wendy's frock straight. "Run down to breaky, pettums. Mummie won't be a minute; she's just got to finish baby Caroline."

She lifted the baby to put on her frock. Her mind pushed away George's words. Nonsense! Of course it wasn't nonsense; George was only talking like that to frighten her.

As a gesture of independence, and as a first step to life on the farm, George left his hat on his head.

"There is a place I know has a list of good billets on farms and such like."

Anna shuddered at this description, but she was determined to bring the conversation to an end. George was in a silly mood; never before had he talked about farms; when they had a holiday they went to Bournemouth, Torquay or Eastbourne. Not the best hotels—alas! they couldn't afford those—but still to hotels of sorts, where they met nice people with children who were suitable companions for their children and where she could sit and talk to other mothers about the Royal Family and what the best people did. They never went away at Easter, and they were not going this year, which, of all years, was out of the question. It was, however, no time to tell George that. Clearly he had got out of bed the wrong side and needed a dose of salts. She smiled at him sweetly.

"You must hurry, dear, or you'll be late. You get that list of addresses from your friend and we'll talk the whole thing over this evening."

Doris, pushing John in his perambulator and with Jimmie trotting by her side, saw Anna and her children coming down the road. Secretly Doris had been suffering from a frailty from which she had supposed herself too intelligent to suffer. She had been jealous. Now she was gloating at Anna's misfortune. She had told herself, Andrew, Mum and Dad-Tring, and anyone else who had mentioned the subject, that if the idea had been put to her that Jimmie or John might be used in a film she would have refused at once. She said she believed that a child should become a useful citizen as soon as possible, but that she was fundamentally opposed to child wage-earners, as it opened the door to old evils and prevented concentration on education. She had not succeeded in making herself believe in the words that her mouth said. It had been humiliating to discover how her heart rose each day when Anna had to report there was no news. She tried to tell herself that it was not that she minded Wendy being picked out, but that it was so bad for Wendy, who was an affected little minx as it was; but she was too intelligent to fool herself that this was the reason. She knew she felt like biting something when she thought of Anna lah-di-dahing it off to a studio in a large car, while she, pushing John in his pram, took Jimmie to school as usual.

This morning there was no need to ask Anna if there was any news. Anna, appalled by George's talk of farms and low-spirited from disappointment, did not look in the least like somebody who had heard good news. She looked, in fact, so wretched that Doris, who disapproved of uprisings of emotion of any sort, found herself sorry for her.

"'Morning, Anna. Cheer up! No morning pram-pushing for five weeks. That's something to be thankful for."

Anna resented being told to cheer up; it suggested there was reason for despondency.

"I'm not depressed. Just a little tired with the spring." Doris walked on briskly, pushing her pram as though it was a tractor carving the way to a new world.

"You need a change. Can't George get a day or two off and take you somewhere nice?"

It was with difficulty that Anna restrained herself. Why had everybody to talk about going away this morning? Could nobody see that at the present time it was impossible for her to get away; that it was imperative that she should be at home? Her easy friendship with Doris was of value to her, so she bit back what she would like to have said; Doris would not stand rough handling from her, any more than she would from Doris. Between them it was impossible to snap out, "Don't be an idiot!" Impossible to trust her far enough to moan, "Why haven't I heard from the film people?" Only real friends could have the relief of being able to confide absolutely anything, the relief that came from unburdening. Frustrated, Anna changed the conversation to the safer one of babies.

Ruth could have borne it if she had not run into her sisters-in-law that morning. Anna and Doris seemed so free from problems. Anna's lovely little Wendy and her big, fine Geoffrey seemed to cause her no worry.

Doris's Jimmie—though Ruth could not imagine why, seeing the way he was raised—seemed an exceptionally easy, uninhibited little boy. Then—lucky girls!—they had babies. Ruth never saw her sisters-in-law's babies without suffering a funny feeling under her heart, as if a hand had clutched her there. Why, oh why didn't she start another baby? Why did her only child have to be a problem, when her sisters-in-law's children were not? Maybe the answer, or at least part of the answer, was the fact that there was more than one child; the author of *The Mind and the Child* had written quite a piece about that, but he had not explained how you started another baby when for no reason a baby refused to start in the ordinary way.

Standing together, the girls made a charming picture. Anna's English fairness, Doris's clear-cut lines and neat, hatless dark head, Ruth's red-gold hair and her general soignée, young-American air; many a mother looked at them as they passed and said to themselves: "Good-looking lot, the three Mrs. Trings."

Actually the conversation between the three Mrs. Trings was extremely halting. Ruth said kindly to Anna that she looked tired. Anna said she was not tired, why should she be? Ruth asked if she had heard from the movie people. Anna replied in a what's-it-got-to-do-with-you voice that she had not. Before Ruth had a chance to say tactfully that Anna must not mind the slowness, movie people were that way, there was always talk about it back home, Doris broke in with, "I'd forget about it, if I were you, Anna."

It was the nearest thing; Anna almost answered, "I daresay you would, but you're not me, your Jimmie is hardly likely to interest film people." Fortunately for their friendship, before the words were spoken the school clock began to growl, which was its preliminary to striking nine, and all three mothers had to shoo their children into the cloakroom.

The last day of each term the mothers were invited by Miss Faulk, the headmistress, into the school for morning prayers, to hear a short programme and the headmistress's report. It was an informal affair, as it had to be, when almost every mother had a restive baby on her knee. The mothers, unless they had a child performing in some outstanding way, only attended as a matter of duty. Each term there were nursery rhymes sung with action, very ill-rehearsed, two or three agitated children were prompted through recitations, there were songs about snowdrops or birdies and, at the end, a performance by the school percussion band. This term Geoffrey was the conductor of the percussion band, Jimmie recited, Paul was one of the performers in the nursery rhymes, Wendy the centre-piece of all the nursery rhymes. The Mrs. Trings should have been pleased, but they were not. Anna was too disgruntled to be pleased about anything. Doris disapproved of the poem Jimmie recited; she did not like to hear him say, "Here a little child I stand, Heaving up my either hand". She thought it a mistake to teach children religious verses. Little children should be taught no religion. They should be free when they were older to take to religion if they wanted to. It aggravated her that the school let him recite that poem of Herrick's. It was aiding and abetting Andrew, who was always murmuring about children's services.

Ruth watched Paul with dismay. If she had not read *The Mind and the Child* and had not been worried about him she would have enjoyed him, as did the other parents. Paul refused to be one of a group; in each nursery rhyme he gave his own very individual performance, and the more the mothers laughed the more he improvised. Ruth's gloom was made deeper when a parent said, "Your little boy is amusing. So original." Ruth knew that her friend, the author of *The Mind and the Child*, would not call Paul's showing off that. She was sure he would say he was an outstanding example of thrashing out by a child who had been forced into too small a mould. She was glad when the performance came to an end and the children were sent off to their classrooms, while the parents listened to Miss Faulk's report.

There was polite applause at the end of the report. The mothers got to their feet. They stood for a moment or two congratulating each other on their children's performances. Miss Faulk made a polite coughing sound to attract attention. She felt happy herself, and this was in her voice. She looked at Ruth.

"Mrs. Tring, would you come to my office for a moment? I have a message for you from that film company who were here the other day."

Ruth supposed the remark was addressed to Anna, who was behind her. She stepped to one side. A silence fell on the other mothers. So Mrs. George Tring had heard about Wendy. Well, wasn't that exciting! They looked at Anna with envy; lucky Mrs. George Tring!

Anna felt a little dizzy. Until that moment she had not realised how faint her hope was growing; it was as if, at the headmistress's word, she had sprung from an illness into perfect health. She even looked different; her skin seemed clearer, her blue eyes brighter, her fair hair more golden. It was no wonder Wendy was such a pretty little thing, thought the mothers, Mrs. George Tring was such a pretty woman; though, they added, if only she didn't have to talk in that silly BBC way.

The mothers moved to each side to make a passage-way for Anna. It was then Miss Faulk remembered some story that one of the camera-men had spoken to Mrs. George Tring about a test for Wendy. Miss Faulk, the only child of a parson overflowing with goodness, if lacking in sufficiency of the wisdom of this world to succeed in it, had been given the gift of a fine home background. One of the results of her training was that she was too well-balanced to waste time on a story of that sort. If she paid attention to possible occurrences she would have no peace. But the letter this morning had to be noticed. She had hoped when she read the name of the film company on the envelope that her school had been selected to be used in a film. It had been a mild disappointment to read it was not her school, but one of her pupils in whom the company were interested. Then she had laughed at herself and thrown off her disappointment. What an egoist she was becoming! What fun this would be for Mrs. Peter Tring! To decide "yes" or "no" would have been a difficult problem if it had concerned an older child, but it would not hurt a baby like Paul; probably it would only mean two or three days' work; and such a change for that pretty little American Mrs. Tring. These, until she saw Anna's face, had been her only thoughts on the subject; then she was humiliated at her stupidity. What had she done? She should have had the imagination to guess that a young mother might have counted on that vague remark about a film test. Evidently Mrs. George Tring had not only counted on it, but now, thinking it to be true, was uplifted as if she were seeing a vision. Why had she spoken of the letter before all the other mothers? So humiliating for the poor girl to find it was not her child but her sister-in-law's in whom the film company were interested. However, it was no good prolonging the agony. She said gently:

"It's not about Wendy, Mrs. George; it's about Paul."

It was dreadful. It made Miss Faulk feel sick to watch the happiness die in Anna's face, and bitterness and resentment take its place. It was no good telling herself that Mrs. George was an idiot to have counted on anything so ephemeral. She had counted on it, and what it meant to her, not only to have her hopes dashed but to see her sister-in-law's child preferred to her own, might just as well have been written, so clearly was it to be read on her face. The situation was not helped by the other mothers. They were chittering like a lot of birds in a hedge.

"Paul!"

"Well, I never!"

"Fancy that!"

"Aren't you excited, Mrs. Peter?"

Ruth was winded with surprise. She did not hear what the other mothers were saying to her. She did not see, or think, of Anna. She did not feel herself pushed forward towards Miss Faulk. Her mind was occupied digesting what had been said. Miss Faulk had heard from the film company. They had sent a message about Paul. It was obviously just some little thing—a test, maybe—but he had been picked out for it from the school. Was that wonderful? It was just the sort of thing the author of *The Mind and the Child* had said was what he needed.

Miss Faulk's heart sank farther. So that nice little American Mrs. Tring was going to be silly too. It was to be expected that pretty, empty-headed Mrs. "Jist-Fency" Tring, as some people unkindly called her, would believe in fairies at the bottom of her garden, but not Mrs. Peter Tring. She looked such a healthy-minded, sensible little creature, it would not have surprised her had the girl laughed at the idea of her son taking part in a film. Yet here she was coming towards her like a sleep-walker, her eyes glittering just as brightly as poor Mrs. George Tring's had done, and her face with the same uplifted expression as of one seeing a vision. It was pathetic! She wished the film unit had never come near her school.

Ruth, dazzled at the sudden help which had come to her, moved blindly forward, and so brushed against Anna. It was a mere jostle, a touching of shoulders, but it was all that was needed to inflame Anna. It was the last indignity. Her hopes had crashed. She was beyond thought or reason. To her Ruth was the cause of her misery. Fortunately for herself, she had been brought up not to raise her voice, and her early training stood by her, so what she said was heard only by Ruth and Miss Faulk.

"What d'you think you're doing? Just because your spoilt little horror of a son gets taken notice of, is that any reason to barge about knocking other people over? Not that there's a chance of Peter letting Paul act in a film. He's worried enough as it is at the way you spoil the child. You ought to hear what everybody says about the idiotic way you go on with him. Everybody says if you are allowed to go on spoiling him he'll turn out a good-for-nothing and it'll be your fault."

Miss Faulk, her face stern, but her heart full of pity, laid a hand on Anna's arm.

"You don't mean what you are saying, my dear, and I'm sure your sister-in-law knows it." She signalled to Ruth to follow her. "Come along, Mrs. Peter."

Doris, though she had not heard what was said, had known from the tenseness of Anna's back and the way her head moved, as if each word were spat from her, that there had been something of a scene. She had struggled for a few seconds with herself. She had reminded herself that she was too intelligent to sink to taking sides in a female squabble, then the revolting picture of Ruth—the perfect Ruth so admired by Mum and Dad-Tring and hers and Anna's husbands—having additional glory because her spoilt brat of a child had been picked by the picture people, got the better of her. The moment Miss Faulk led Ruth into her office she joined Anna, and said something which spared Anna the final degradation of bursting into tears.

"That so-and-so will need keeping in her place."

Miss Faulk sat down at her desk and motioned Ruth into a chair. She unlocked a drawer, and took out a large envelope and passed it to Ruth. In the envelope was a letter and a photograph. The letter-paper was crisp and rich-looking; across the top in enormous letters was printed "Rose of England Films Incorporated", and underneath in smaller letters the names of the directors of the company. The letter was signed "William Dragon".

"Dear Madam,

One of our camera-men took the enclosed picture outside your school. It is not very clear, I am afraid, as the light was bad and it is just blown up from a frame; but we should be most grateful if you could give us the name and address of the parents of the child in the enclosed photograph. We have put a pencilled circle round his picture. We are shortly making a film in which there is a part for a small boy, and we feel this may be the right child."

Ruth looked at the photograph. It was not a good picture; it was dim and seemed to have lines across it. But there was the school door and, in front of it, Wendy, Jimmie and Paul. Paul was outlined by a pencilled circle.

"It's very like him, though he looks kind of scared."

"Doesn't he? He's got a very speaking little face, but you would think he was escaping from brigands or Red Indians. I suppose really he was concentrating on getting down the steps, or perhaps it's just a bad photograph. I suppose that blown-up photographs come out like that," Miss Faulk laughed. "What extraordinary expressions they use! It's nothing to do with me, but was there any truth in what Mrs. George said? Is there no chance of his father allowing him to act in a film?"

The letter had far exceeded Ruth's hopes. She had not dreamed there would be more than a test, and had been prepared for that to come to nothing. But if there was a part for a small boy and the film was to be made shortly, then there was a possibility that Paul might be given the part. To act in a film was something that no other child had done; it was surely the answer to prayer, the compensation he needed to cure him of his feeling of loss of protection. It would win him more than approval, it would make quite a local celebrity of him. It would be the finish of his need to keep searching round for an outlet; the outlet was here, in this letter. If he got this little part he would start right away growing up a reasoned, normal, uninhibited boy.

"It won't be easy. I figure Peter might say 'no'; but I shall not allow that to make any difference. If the offer to play a part is made, why then, Paul shall play it."

Miss Faulk liked independence; it was love of independence that had made her, on coming into a little capital, throw up her career as a teacher of literature to become head of a kindergarten.

"I like your spirit, but I'm afraid it won't be as easy as that. I imagine the consent of both parents will be needed."

Ruth shifted from Paul's problems as presented by her friend, the author of *The Mind and the Child*, and turned her thoughts to Peter. At once she accepted that the chance of his agreeing to Paul being in a movie was so remote as to be almost unimaginable. This would mean a fight—a fight that she had to win. Paul was a baby with all his life before him, a life which it was in her power to straighten out; Peter was her husband, whom she worshipped, but he was a grown man, normal, not in the least in need of straightening. Whatever it cost, Paul must come first.

Miss Faulk had been watching Ruth's face. Her uneasiness grew. She wished she had burned the wretched letter. She spoke with caution, for it was not her business to interfere and she did not want to risk a snub, which might make it impossible should the need arise, for the girl to treat her as a friend.

"There are two sides to this business; I can imagine many fathers would dislike film acting for their sons . . ."

Ruth leant forward.

"You must forgive me interrupting, but this is more serious than you realise. Paul has been causing me some anxiety. I would have liked to have had him psychoanalysed, but I do not know of a good psycho-analyst. I have instead had the practical help of a very wise writer on mental hygiene. You don't come in contact with the very little children, but I believe Paul's teacher has no trouble with him while he is in school; but at home I have been deeply anxious. There have been too many screaming attacks; sometimes he holds his breath, frequently he shows off."

It was with difficulty that Miss Faulk held back the word "spoilt".

"And what does the writer on mental hygiene suggest these things point to?"

Ruth gravely explained about the Tring mould, thrashing out, need for compensation, a house divided, and the danger of neurotic infantilism.

"I realise, Miss Faulk, that my sister-in-law, Mrs. George Tring, was speaking in temper; but you can imagine how I felt when I heard her say that if little Paul turned out a no-good it would be my fault. Those words may have been said in temper, Miss Faulk, but they are true."

Miss Faulk had met many fanatics in her life, but a mother like Ruth had not come her way before. She accepted there were children who needed their minds attended to by a doctor, but she was sure a baby of Paul's age was not one of them. Poor Mrs. George Tring had been right, probably, when she had said all she had about spoiling. It was a new idea to cure a spoilt child by sending him to a psycho-analyst. However, that his mother believed her child needed help, and that acting in a film would give it to him, there could be no doubt. She must go carefully. This mother would be more difficult to argue with than the ordinary silly, ambitious type.

"If that's how you feel, I must hope you get a part for Paul. If you think it your duty to do so, I hope you can persuade your husband to see your viewpoint; but, if you can't, don't be too disappointed, my dear. Try not to set your mind too much on this film chance. After all, Paul's only a baby, plenty of other"—Miss Faulk felt for the word—"compensations will turn up."

Ruth was planning ahead. She had already in her mind left Miss Faulk's office. She picked up the letter and photograph and, putting them back in their envelope, got up.

"I will borrow these, if I may. Thank you for your kindness. Good morning."

Miss Faulk went to a window. It looked towards the gate to the road. She watched Ruth come down the school steps. The girl's head was up. She walked briskly down the path and out of the gate. Miss Faulk watched her until she reached the corner. "She might be Joan of Arc guided by voices," she thought. "What a pity they are not guiding her in a more useful direction."

Emma, from the front bedroom, saw Ruth come up the street. "Dearie me," she thought, "something's up, or Ruth wouldn't be walking that fast just to call on me."

There was, however, no sign of anxiety about her as she opened the door.

"Well, dear, this is nice! A lovely surprise. Come in; I'll soon have a cup of coffee ready. It won't be like yours," but Ruth stopped her.

"I don't want coffee, thank you. I want to talk to you, and maybe get your help." She felt suddenly that rushing in uninvited, demanding a talk, was un-British. "It's your fault I'm here. It was what you said about how you worked Dad-Tring round to thinking something you wanted was what he wanted that made me visit you."

Emma led the way into the front room. She picked up her knitting-bag. If you could not have cups in your hands, then the next best way of making a daughter-in-law feel at ease was to knit, while she talked. There was something cosy about the click of knitting-needles. She sat back in an armchair, smoothed her overall, pulled the sock she was knitting out of her bag, and settled back.

"Well, dear?"

The moment Ruth had thought of talking to Mum-Tring she had planned what she would say. She would explain events in their order. It was no good giving her a back-to-front picture, she had to see the facts as they had happened.

Emma, knitting away, tried to follow what Ruth was saying. Many of the words she used were too difficult for her, but evidently she had been right when she had guessed Paul was causing trouble between his parents. She expected Peter was right in putting down Paul's attack, which Ruth had described, to spoiling; but that did not mean Emma sided with Peter. It sounded to her a very silly book that Ruth had got hold of, but if she did not like Peter's ideas of discipline she had a right to her own opinion. Of course she would have to work Peter round tactfully, but it could be done. She had no idea what this talk of compensation was about. She had never heard of that; still, if Ruth thought Paul needed anything she ought to find a way to give it him. Knitting placidly, turning over what Ruth was saying, wondering how to help, Emma was not prepared for the end of the story. Helping Ruth to get her own way about Paul was one thing, but hearing Ruth's side of what was bound to develop into a family row was quite another. When Ruth described what Miss Faulk had said at the end of the school entertainment, Emma's tongue, without her intention, clicked against her teeth.

"Tch! tch! Oh, dear! Was Anna there?"

Ruth, sticking closely to Paul's case-history, was surprised.

"Why, yes. I wasn't going to tell you that. She seemed a mite upset, but it was just nothing. She didn't mean a word she said. Now I must show you the letter."

Emma read the letter, but she barely took in what it said. She had seen George and, though Wendy's film chances had not been discussed, she had known he was having a bad time at home. He looked worn and miserable. Not that her sympathies over the film were entirely with George. She knew poor silly Anna was discontented. She thought it foolish to let a child act in a film, but if it was going to make Anna easier to live with she hoped it would happen. George was her eldest, and, though she loved all her boys, he had been the first to lie under her heart, and her senses had never let her forget it. The possible results of this letter swam between Emma's eye and the paper. Anna would feel very bitter about this. She had counted on this film to make people look up to her. It was natural she wanted to mix, and for her children to mix, with her own kind, though Emma could have told her no part in a film would make that happen. It was just foolishness to suppose it would. All the same, that was what Anna believed, just as she would be believing now that people were tittering behind her back at her disappointment, though there might be a bit of truth in that. Anna would be so upset she would want to hit out at everybody. Poor George would get it first. Emma's heart missed a beat at that thought. People like themselves married for better or worse, but you couldn't tell with a girl like Anna: properly upset she might say something foolish and run off; not that she was likely to leave the children, but you couldn't count on her.

Ruth was hurt by the long pause. She had counted more than she had realised on Mum-Tring's help and understanding. She held out her hand.

"I guess you must know that letter by heart. Anyway, I must be going; I have taken up too much of your morning."

Emma was shocked at herself. Poor Ruth! she had not thought about her; only about Anna. It was very wrong of her, especially as Ruth was a foreigner with no mother to discuss things with. It was good of her to come to her instead. And what a way she had treated her! She handed back the letter.

"You must forgive me, dearie. Do you know what I was thinking, which just shows what a selfish old mother-in-law you've got? I was thinking of family rows."

"You mean Peter will make a row?"

Emma had not got around to Peter. She sighed.

"He will, but I was thinking of Anna. You see, dear, this isn't a very big town, and we're pretty well known here. Anna's never taken to the place, and so she isn't as well liked as some. She'll feel there's some pleased to see her get a slap in the face, and there's truth in it. I've always counted myself a lucky woman to have all my sons and their families close to me, but when something like this happens I wish you all lived farther apart. It's human nature to feel sorry for the one that's down, so Doris is likely to side with Anna, which means taking sides against you." Without knowing it, a mixture of scorn and pity put an edge on her voice. "What Doris thinks, Andrew will think. You've always got on well with Dad-Tring, but he'll be against you in this too, and so, if he's got any sense, will George."

"I'm not afraid of being unpopular with the family if what I am doing is right for Paul."

Emma looked at Ruth. She could see that this was true. She saw what Miss Faulk had seen, only to her Ruth did not look like Joan of Arc hearing voices, but an impetuous girl who might do something silly unless an older woman could stop her, if that older woman could see a way to it without seeming to interfere.

"Peter isn't going to be easy about this, dear. Acting in pictures isn't a thing the Trings hold with. You ought to have heard the way Dad-Tring carried on when he thought little Wendy might be going to get an offer. Peter's a proper Tring, you know."

Ruth jumped up and knelt at Emma's feet. She laid her arms on Emma's knees and gazed up into her face.

"You said you couldn't force a Tring, but you could work them round to thinking differently. Tell me the way to handle this. Now I've told you why I want it, you do see how important it is, don't you? You are with me, aren't you?"

Emma laid down her knitting, she stroked Ruth's hair. "I'm not against you, child. I don't understand really what you mean about Paul. I daresay I'm old-fashioned, but I don't see children as problems. But I understand that you do, and that you want this for Paul because you think it will be good for him. I wish that letter had never reached you. It's going to make bad trouble all round. But the letter has reached you, and I see you mean to act on it, so now there's nothing for it but for us to put on our thinking caps and see the best way for you to set about it."

"I reckon that the mothers from the school will be getting places, I expect one of them will have run to Tring's. Should I go there right away and show Peter the letter and tell him straight out that I am answering it?"

"No, I wouldn't do that, dear. There's three Trings there, remember. You don't want to take on three at once when you needn't." There was a silence while both pondered. Suddenly Emma came to a decision. "You go and telephone. Film-people are sure to be on the tele-phone. You ask them when they can see you and Paul. If you catch a fast train, it's only an hour to London. They've only seen that one picture; it may be when they see Paul they'll find he won't do. You needn't say anything to anybody until you know if they want him. I never hold with crossing bridges before you come to them."

"You mean take Paul without telling Peter he's going?"

"Yes. What harm'll that do? Go on, telephone now."

The telephone was in the passage. Ruth left the front room door ajar so that Emma could hear what was said.

Ruth did not like telephoning the film company. She would rather have written. She felt telephoning seemed rushing things and invited a snub.

It seemed that at the film offices a girl must sit right on top of the telephone, for at the first buzz a high, mechanical voice recited:

"Rose of England Films Incorporated."

Ruth asked for Mr. William Dragon. There was silence, then another equally mechanised female voice said: "Mr. Dragon's secretary speaking. What name, please?"

Ruth had not been stenographer to Mr. Sholtz for nothing. She wasted no time, but in the fewest possible words summed up the reason for her call. The result at the other end of the line was startling. There was nothing mechanised about the voice which answered.

"Oh, Mrs. Tring; you're the mother of that little boy in the photograph. Mr. Dragon will be so pleased you rang. He's in conference, but I'll send a message in to him right away. I think, Mrs. Tring, he would be glad if you could bring the little boy to see him as soon as possible. I'm just looking at Mr. Dragon's engagements. I suppose you couldn't manage this afternoon? You could? Well, I'll send a note now to Mr. Dragon, if you'll hold on. Would three do? We'll send a car, of course."

Ruth put her hand over the receiver and called to Emma.

"She thinks Mr. Dragon would like us to go at three o'clock to-day. They'll send a car."

Emma joined Ruth in the passage. She spoke in a whisper, for she never trusted telephones.

"A car! Don't let it come to the door, dearie. It's bound to cause talk. Whatever you've got to say to Peter you'd rather he heard it from you than from gossip from the neighbours."

"I'll have them pick us up in the car park. We shan't be noticed there." Ruth heard the secretary returning. "Yes, I'm here . . ."

Ruth came back into the sitting-room.

"I don't know whether it shows, Mum-Tring, but your daughter-in-law feels about two inches taller than when she got up this morning. There is something very soothing about being made to feel important." She kissed Emma. "I'm going to get Paul from school right away. He'll need his rest early, and if I go now I'll not have to meet Anna and Doris. If I did they'd be sure to ask what was in the letter, and I just hate to tell lies."

Emma kissed her.

"Good-bye, dear. I'm not going to pretend I hope they want Paul, I don't, but I do want anything that makes you happy. Anyway, enjoy this afternoon and try not to count on the result too much. If they don't want him in the film I'm sure we can make a fuss of him some other way."

Ruth laid her face against Emma's.

"One thing I will say: I hope I do nothing to worry you. I'd surely hate that to happen, for you are just the sweetest mother-in-law."

Emma watched Ruth go down the road. She laid her hand against her face where the girl's cheek had rubbed against it.

"Bless her! Nothing to worry me! I feel the storm rising."

CHAPTER 3
ROSE OF ENGLAND FILMS INCORPORATED

RUTH had pictured the offices of the Rose of England Films Incorporated as looking very much like Mr. Sholtz's office. They could not have been less like. The company had taken over as offices premises which had once been a great London house. Instead of being whisked up several floors in an elevator, Ruth and Paul climbed what had once been the grand staircase. At the top, where once famous hosts and hostesses had received their guests, there stood Mr. Dragon's secretary, Miss Mona Bun. Mona Bun's life had arranged itself just as she wished it to be arranged. Her father was a stonemason, and her mother not only a housewife who had brought six children into the world, but also a lay preacher. Each Bun son and daughter, as they grew up, showed that they were the child of their parents. They were religious in a narrow, fervent way. The sons became stonemasons. The girls married men who did heavy manual work, and they bore them plenty of children. Mona was different; she hid that she was different, for that would lead to unpleasantness, and her ability to see in advance what would lead to unpleasantness and avoid it was one of her talents. She won a scholarship, which, as her father said, though uncalled for, could do no harm, and, due to the higher education provided by the scholarship, won another at a secretarial college. From the secretarial college, out of which she passed with faster shorthand than any employer wished to use, she took a post at a missionary college. "Very nice too," said her parents, which was just what Mona had hoped they would say. "All unpleasantness avoided," she thought, "and at the same time getting them used to me living away from home." Every two or three years Mona had changed her posts.

"Bettering herself' was how she described it to her parents. She went from missionaries to books, from books to finance, from finance to photography, and then, convinced that her family had ceased to ask exactly what she did, she moved, slowly at first but always steadily, towards her present job with Mr. Dragon. For Mona had a feeling for romance. She wanted none for herself, but she could not see enough happening to other people. She read nothing but true-life romances. Her treats were standing outside buildings inside which, or out of which, would walk the romantic figures of the moment. In her work there was romance—not enough, for Mona could never have enough romance; and there were too many boys and girls who raised her hopes when, as nobodies, they seemed headed to be somebodies, but too often something went wrong and back they slipped, the worse for their experience, to being nobodies again. Mona did not brood on failures—hers was a nature of utter optimism—but she did pray each day that something wonderful would happen (where she could see it) to somebody. To-day it had. Though her face did not show it, her heart was soft with happiness as she watched Ruth and Paul climbing towards her. She could have sung, she was so pleased for them, "Heigho, heigho, on the way to Romance they go."

What she actually said was:

"Mrs. Tring? Mr. Dragon will see you and the little boy right away."

*

Doris had found herself in the unaccustomed position of mopper-up of tears and confidante of a girl friend. It had started after Anna's outburst at Ruth by her asking her to come in for a cup of tea. This was partly good-heartedness and partly a wish to talk of the awful effect on Paul's character of his being allowed to act in a film. Anna, however, having reached near privacy, went to pieces. No sooner was she in Doris's kitchen than she flung herself into a chair, buried her face in her arms on the table and sobbed. Between sobs she gulped out her sorrows. Doris heard some of the things Anna had counted on as a result of Wendy making a film. She heard how awful all the Tring circle were, except, of course, Doris (even in the middle of a crying jag Anna remembered to say that). Doris heard how snooty many parents were, and how their snootiness hurt. She heard a tirade against Ruth that went on and on. As Anna moaned, Doris's annoyance at Ruth's Paul having been picked out over her Jimmie evaporated. Anna's head being buried, she could not see Doris's expression, which was a mercy, for it was one of disgust. Everything that Anna was moaning about was to Doris the type of middle-class reactionary nonsense which she despised and hoped to live to see erased from the mind of man. However had she and Anna become friends? The girl was a moron! Anna, unconscious of Doris's thoughts, lifted her head.

"Oh goodness! Whatever must I look like? It'll soon be time to fetch the children."

"The kettle's just boiling; you'll feel better when you've had a cup of tea. I'll pick up Geoffrey and Wendy for you, but you'll have to look after John if I do; the children always have such a lot to bring home the last day of term I can't carry their things and push his pram."

This brought on a fresh stream of tears from Anna.

"Last day of term! I haven't told you. George wants to take us all away."

Doris made a pot of tea.

"I should think that's a good idea."

"But you don't know where. A farm! A horrible, muddy, lonely farm in Devonshire, full of cows; and I'm terrified of cows."

Doris patted Anna's shoulder. She did it awkwardly, for she was not given to patting.

"Here's your tea. Come on, drink it. It will do you good."

The tea did stop Anna's immediate tears, but it was with relief that Doris set off for the school. She was glad of the walk. Anna's talk and unrestrained crying had made her feel in need of a lot of fresh air. Whatever had she let herself in for? she wondered; and Anna thought she sympathised with all that retrograde nonsense. It was too much.

Outside the school the mothers gathered round her.

"Where was Mrs. George?"

"Isn't Mrs. Peter excited?"

"Won't you feel grand if you have a film-star nephew, Mrs. Andrew?"

Doris looked at them. They were more disgusting than Anna. They were like a lot of animals snapping at some defenceless creature that had fallen down. She disliked the word "masses", and never used it. In her creed every human being was growing towards world citizenship. Every woman was the equal of every man. Every woman had the brain to use a vote intelligently. This yattering mob threatened these beliefs; these creatures had not advanced beyond savagery.

"My sister-in-law is looking after my John as well as her Caroline, so that my hands are free to help the children carry back their things. Mrs. Peter will presumably be here in a moment, so you can ask her yourselves if she's excited. I hope my nephew doesn't become a film star, as I disapprove of children wage-earners."

Doris knew, as she walked away, what the mothers were whispering to each other. She realised they had not taken her words as a snub, but as proof that she was jealous; that she was as mad as Anna that it was Ruth's Paul who had interested the film world; but at that moment she did not mind. Poor, ignorant, gossiping fools! Let them think what they liked.

The children had no sooner rushed out of school than Doris heard how Ruth had come early to fetch Paul.

"Was it because Paul's going to act in a film, Aunty Doris?" Geoffrey asked.

Jimmie, sticking to his training, shouted: "'Course not, silly. Paul's spoilt. He couldn't act in a film, could he, Mum?"

Wendy smiled seraphically.

"Mumsy says I'm going to act in a film."

Geoffrey, who was ahead, pranced back.

"If Paul acts in a film, will it be instead of Wendy?"

"Yes, I should think so. Your mother thought they wanted Wendy; but, as it's Paul they want to see, I expect it means they want a boy."

Wendy looked up at her aunt.

"They must be very silly to want Paul, mustn't they?"

"I think the whole idea's silly, whether it's you or Paul. Children should be learning lessons, not wasting time making films."

Geoffrey and Wendy gazed at her round-eyed. Geoffrey said severely:

"That isn't what Mummy thinks."

Doris refused to discuss the matter further, and the children ran on ahead. She wished she had not snubbed the mothers. It would have been more dignified to have ignored them. Now that her rage had passed she was sorry she had climbed so publicly on to the same side of the fence as Anna. In no time a garbled version of what she had said would be round the town, and one of the first places at which it would be retailed was Tring's. Why had Ruth fetched Paul out of school early? Could she possibly have gone to see the film people already? If so, they were on the edge of a major family row. Dad-Tring had made no secret of what he thought when the idea of Wendy acting in a film had been mooted; he was likely to feel far more strongly about a grandson. Of the three Tring sons, Peter was most obviously a chip off the Tring block; he was unlikely to consider the idea of a son acting in a picture, though he was so crazy about Ruth it was possible she might talk him round. While with his father and brother, Andrew would take the Tring view. In ordinary circumstances she would have made him see sense when he got home. She disapproved of family ties, especially family points of view; each individual should think for himself; it was reactionary and middle-class to stick to the family unit. This time it wouldn't be so easy to say all that. Andrew would have heard, "I'm afraid Mrs. Andrew was a bit upset. No wonder, her being so friendly with Mrs. George; and Mrs. George must be very disappointed—quite set on the idea for little Wendy, I hear she was." There had never been a real family row since she married Andrew; but she had carefully trained him for the day when they were the centre of one. If Andrew ever stood for the Council there was bound to be trouble, for she would divorce him before she allowed him to stand as a Conservative. Then there was the question of church. Already Dad-Tring was getting at Andrew; he had been a sidesman at the parish church for years, and it was surprising that the fact that she had allowed neither Jimmie nor John to be christened had not been mentioned to her, but she knew it had to Andrew, and that he was being got at to send Jimmie to Sunday school. She had planned that they should keep out of any family argument that might arrive—an argument centring round themselves would be all they needed to worry about. Now that it smelt as if a family row was brewing she had let herself get mixed up in it. Blast all the family! especially Ruth, whose fault it would be if there was trouble.

In a room which had once been a ballroom, across a vast desk, Ruth faced Mr. Dragon. At the end of the room Miss Bun sat on the floor helping Paul build card-castles; Mr. Dragon had arranged that Paul faced him, and his eyes seldom left the child for long.

Mr. Dragon was in his way an artist. His father was a teacher of elocution and, had he wished, might have made a name as a stage producer. His mother was a Pole who had been trained as a violinist. It had been their ambition that their only child should be an artist of some sort. William had not at first felt a talent pulling him in any especial direction. He played the violin a bit, he acted a bit, he produced a bit; then Fate led him into a film studio, and at once he had known what he should be at. His gift was not directing pictures, but in seeing what would make a picture and who should be used in its making. Although neither Ruth nor Miss Faulk had heard of him, his was a name rising with every picture he produced.

"Have you read a book, Mrs. Tring, called *Cast a Stone*?"

Ruth shook her head.

"You must; Miss Bun will give you a copy before you leave. I have bought that story. Noel Water will direct it." Mr. Dragon paused for Ruth to show interest in the great name. Ruth had little chance to go to the pictures, and so had not heard of Noel Water, but when working for Mr. Sholtz she had learned to react to expectant pauses. She made her face register interest and delight. "The story is for Nicholas Dram."

Nobody, however little they knew about films, not even a judge, could fail to have heard of Nicholas Dram. Ruth had no need to use her Sholtz office technique, her face without trouble registered interest.

"Nicholas Dram!"

"I bought *Cast a Stone* because there is a great part for him—Jonathan Bone." Mr. Dragon opened a drawer and took out some large photographs. He passed them across to Ruth. "There he is. Do you suppose when he was a child he looked at all like Paul?"

Ruth studied the well-known face: the deep-set, shadowed eyes; the sensitive, delicate features; the hair that must have been once moonlight fair.

"It's difficult to say, but he might. I should guess Mr. Dram had very much Paul's colouring when he was little."

"He had. This story is laid during the adult life of Jonathan Bone. The book showed how he became the man he did, and the film sticks more or less to the same story. As you will see when you read the book, those parts where Jonathan goes back to his life as a small, unwanted boy are very important."

"Unwanted! I shouldn't let Paul act a child that was unwanted."

Mr. Dragon was studying Paul's mobile little face.

"You needn't worry about that if Paul plays little Jonathan; we'll see he doesn't feel unwanted. We had not planned to use so small a boy. Nicholas Dram has a son of twelve who is the image of his father, and we are using him in most of the childhood sequences, but the adapter of the book feels—and he has convinced myself and Noel Water that he's right—that we must have some early sequences, or the story becomes lop-sided." He raised his voice. "Paul, would you come here a minute?"

Paul scrambled up from the floor and ran across the room. He leant against Ruth's chair.

"Mum, Miss Bun has birds what come and eat off her window-sill. She doesn't just give them bread like us, but special seeds. Simply thousands come every day."

"Not thousands, dear," Ruth corrected, "but a lot, I expect."

Mr. Dragon had obviously not read *The Mind and the Child*. He apparently saw no harm in exaggeration.

"What fun if it was thousands! Listen, Paul. I want to tell you a story. There was once a little boy just about your age. His name was Jonathan. He had no mother and no father, and he went to live with people who thought it would be nice to adopt a little boy; but when they had adopted him they found they didn't want him."

"Why? Was he naughty?"

"No. Just ordinary, but they didn't understand that boys can't help being noisy and making a mess sometimes. So what do you think Jonathan did?"

"What?"

"He made up nice people to live with, instead of the nasty ones who were really there."

"What were the nice ones like?"

"Only Jonathan saw them, but people saw him talk to them. Do you ever make up people and talk to them?"

"There's somethin' lives in our house what's very rude. Do you know, it makes noises like this: pouff—pouff, like a very loud noise your inside sometimes makes."

Ruth was going to explain that Paul was talking of the cistern, but with a gesture Mr. Dragon stopped her.

"The people Jonathan made up weren't rude to him; they were very polite. They were so polite they never argued with him, but said 'Aren't you wonderful, Jonathan?' 'Aren't you clever, Jonathan?' 'We think you are the cleverest boy in the world.' In the end he grew up to believe everything they said was true." Mr. Dragon looked across at Miss Bun. "I think Paul would like some tea. Would you, Paul?"

"I drink milk."

"I meant milk. What would you like to eat? Cake and ice-cream?"

Paul turned shining eyes on Ruth.

"Ice-cream! Oh, Mum!"

Mr. Dragon watched the child leave the room with Miss Bun.

"There will have to be tests, of course, and I must see what Noel Water thinks; but I believe we have a find in your boy. He has a very expressive face. When he was telling me that story about something at home . . ."

"The cistern."

"The cistern, was it? His eyes were full of fright. It was that which struck us in that picture I sent you. We're making some of this film outside, and a unit has been round looking for locations. Noel Water saw a run through of schools we might use, and that was where he spotted Paul. He said he had a hunch that he was what we were looking for, and he's good at hunches. Funnily enough, the camera-man was going to show us that very picture because of the little girl; but I don't want a girl, and those sort of pretty-pretty children are two a penny."

"My!" thought Ruth, "what would Anna say if she could hear that?"

"You spoke of a test, Mr. Dragon. What would that mean?"

"I shall ask you to bring Paul to our studios. They are outside London in the direction of where you live. We shall send a car for you, of course. It's urgent we should get little Jonathan cast, so I'll get Miss Bun to fix it for tomorrow, if that suits you."

"A test would mean you would take pictures of Paul to see if he would be right? It wouldn't mean that anything was settled, would it?"

"No, of course not. If he is right, then we shall communicate with you and your husband making an offer; but you sound doubtful. It's no good our making a test if you think you might decide against allowing your boy to play the part."

Ruth thought rapidly. Should she tell this nice Mr. Dragon about how Peter might react? She decided against it. Miraculously just what the author of *The Mind and the Child* thought Paul needed looked like being offered to him. To make Peter see what was right was her business. Nothing would be gained by troubling Mr. Dragon; she would handle everything herself.

"If Paul is the boy you want, then you shall have him."

Mr. Dragon smiled.

"Good." He pressed a button and spoke into a loud-speaker telephone. "Miss Bun, Mrs. Tring is on her way down; when she has had tea I want you to fix with Mr. Water a time for a test tomorrow." He turned back to Ruth. "Good-bye. I shan't see you to-morrow, but I have a feeling we shall meet quite often in the future. You aren't hesitating, are you? You and your husband would like Paul to play this part?"

Ruth, sure of her duty, answered with great confidence.

"There is no hesitation. I repeat what I said before. If you want Paul you shall have him."

Doris had been right when she had guessed that the mothers would not be able to spread the story of Ruth's news, and her own and Anna's reactions to it, quickly enough. One after another they had hurried to the shop, either with the excuse that they had run out of something, or admitting why they had come.

"I just had to pop in, Mr. Peter, to tell you and Mr. Andrew the news . . ."

Dad-Tring had gone solidly on with his job. Business was not built by snubbing customers, even a parcel of yattering women who had only come in to gossip. His weather-beaten, tough, cliffs-of-Dover face showed no sign of his inward scorn. He had been a bit silent, but that was not unusual. Dad-Tring was not one to talk unless he had something he thought it was worth while saying. Once when opportunity had offered he had caught Peter's eye and had given him a wink, but otherwise he might not have heard what was being said. Nor, when dinnertime had come round, had he made immediate reference to the gossip. He had shouted as usual to his two girl employees to warn them that the Tring family were about to eat, had gone outside to wash, come to the table and was half-way through his plateful of pie and had drunk half his beer, before, grinning broadly, he had looked at Peter.

"Feelin' the proud father?"

Peter had grinned back.

"I could hardly keep my face when they were telling me. Lot of fools! Never seemed to strike them Ruth and I mightn't want our boy to be an actor."

Andrew had taken a gulp of beer.

"They said Ruth seemed in a great state about it."

Peter had given an amused snort.

"Lot of foolishness! You know Ruth."

Andrew had not felt too happy. He did not like Doris's name being brought in.

"They said Ruth took Paul out of school early."

Dad-Tring had shaken his head at Andrew.

"They say—If you listen to all the women tell you, you'll find yourself headed for an asylum before you're through."

Andrew had helped himself to cheese.

"You can laugh, Dad; but I don't like the sound of things. I know those gossips would say anything, but I reckon that there has been some sort of letter about Paul and none about Wendy. All the women said that, and if it's true it's going to mean trouble for poor old George. Anna's properly set on this film business."

Dad-Tring had helped himself to cheese and radishes. "That's George's funeral. Anna's only a silly bit of a girl; he shouldn't let her get fancified notions. Pictures! Film-actin'! Disgustin'! I don't see Peter here lettin' Ruth get set on any such foolishness."

Peter had chewed contentedly.

"I don't have to bother. Ruth's laughing at the idea." Andrew had lit a cigarette.

"I hope you're right to take it so calmly. I must say I don't like the sound of things. We know it isn't your fault or Ruth's if Paul's picked out instead of Wendy, but Anna won't see it that way. You know what damn-fool ideas women get."

For a moment neither Dad-Tring nor Peter had answered; both knew the other's thoughts. No woman had more damn-fool ideas than Doris. Dad-Tring had given Andrew a sharp look.

"Anna will have to get over it. There's no need for you to worry. "Doris won't care, will she?"

Andrew had stabbed at the table with a match.

"Doris won't care for herself—wouldn't want Jimmie or John anywhere near a film studio—but she's thick with Anna." Dad-Tring had snorted. Andrew had looked at him. "I don't want to meet trouble half-way, but you know what it is when women get together."

Dad-Tring had taken his pipe out of his pocket and filled it slowly. Filling a pipe was a pleasant occupation not to be hurried.

"Doris is your affair, son, just as Anna is George's. I only know I never remember a time when your mother got foolish ideas or got together with other women, and I would bet that Peter never knows it with Ruthie. But I'll give you a bit of advice. If your Doris thinks she's got to back up Anna in this business, you give her somethin' else to think about."

"What?"

Dad-Tring had pondered.

"You might do worse than see about gettin' your boys christened. Never heard the like—a boy of four and a half not christened! Even little John ought to have been christened months back."

Andrew was ashamed to have unchristened offspring, but not yet ashamed enough to fight Doris on the subject. He had scowled.

"We'll get them done later on. I'm working Doris round to the idea."

Dad-Tring had winked at Peter.

"That's good news. But if you find she's full of Anna's troubles, you change the subject to christenin's; that'll stop her." He had paused to light his pipe. "In the ordinary way I don't like to interfere in your affairs, son; but not being christened is different. You were all brought up properly. It worries your mother and me."

Andrew had got up.

"Well, I wish you'd stop worrying. Doris will have them christened when she feels like it."

Andrew had slammed out of the room. Peter had looked after him sympathetically.

"Poor old Andrew! I bet he'll have hell from Doris if he tries to talk her round."

Dad-Tring had puffed at his pipe.

"More fool him! I've no patience with him or George. To hear Andrew, you'd think the world was comin' to an end because Anna's disappointed about that film. If I had my way I'd take a slipper to both Anna and Doris to teach 'em to do as they're told, same as your mother and Ruthie. You didn't have any nonsense about Paul's christenin', and you won't be hearin' any nonsense about this film-actin', and if there was you'd soon put a stop to it."

Peter had been thinking of Ruth. She would just have cleared away the lunch-things. After his rest she would take young Paul for a walk. Happiness and contentment flowed through him.

"Too right, I won't. But Ruth's a girl in a million, bless her."

Ruth telephoned Emma to tell her the result of her visit to Mr. Dragon. Emma, though she kept her feelings from her voice, was thankful to hear that nothing was settled.

"You keep Peter off the subject to-night, dear. He's sure to have heard the news at the shop."

"I'll have to tell him if he asks right out."

"He won't, dear. It wouldn't be like him. Trings don't ask right out about things they might not like to hear. He'll hint round, but you put him off. Time enough when you know what this test comes to. But put Paul to bed early;

it'll do him good after such an afternoon, and he's bound to tell his father he rode in a car, if nothing else." When Peter came home Paul was in bed and Ruth preparing his supper. He kissed Ruth.

"Where's Paul?"

"In bed and asleep, I hope, so don't go up."

"Why's he gone to bed early?"

"Seemed tired. It's been quite a day. He was in all the nursery rhymes at the school breaking-up show."

Peter hovered in the doorway.

"What sort of a day have you had?"

Ruth smiled at him.

"Fine. The seeds you've got under glass want watering." As he fetched his water-can Peter whistled. He had known he was right when he had told Dad and Andrew Ruth would pay no attention to the letter, but it was good to find how right. He put the film out of his mind. Home was the place where life went on undisturbed. Ruth singing in the kitchen, Paul around somewhere, himself doing a job of watering, or maybe listening to the radio, or reading the paper. It was all he wanted; he was lucky, and he knew it.

Anna, though she was pale, had hidden the signs of her tears. To avoid the risk of Geoffrey or Wendy mentioning Paul's film chance to their father she had given them a treat. Recklessly she had dived into the sugar and fat ration so that they might make toffee. It was unlikely, unless he had run into his father, Andrew or Peter, that George would have heard anything; and he must not hear. If he knew that no letter was coming about Wendy, that would settle this awful farm idea. Somehow she must stave that off. A farm at any time would be terrible, but feeling as wretched as she did now, it would be the end.

As it happened, George did not want to mention the farm that night. He had told Anna they were going to a farm, and that would be that. He could see she was going to be tiresome, full of excuses, like waiting for that letter about Wendy; but that would not alter his decision that they would go away. What might change his plans was that he had learned from a friend that it was not a good time of year for the sort of things he wanted to do. It seemed most creatures would be breeding and could not be shot or caught. A place miles from anywhere would be fine, but he would have liked something to do; it was a pity about the close season for coarse fishing. It might be fun to give the farmer a hand. He had never done anything of that sort, and there was a lot to do this time of year; fine for the kids; good to get down to the earth and watch things grow, but he would have to find the right place; until then he would keep off the holiday and let Anna get used to the idea that they were going before he brought the plan up again.

Doris and Andrew fenced round the subject of Paul, both anxious to find out what the other knew and felt, and both equally anxious not to mention it. Their efforts were spoilt by Jimmie.

"Paul's goin' to act in a film, Dad, instead of Wendy."

Andrew looked at Doris.

"I heard something. Is it true?"

Doris gave an impatient shrug of her shoulders.

"How should I know? I haven't got second sight, have I? I should hope Peter wouldn't let him; he's spoilt enough as it is."

Andrew could see he had to tread carefully. When she was in this mood it was like living with a firework instead of a wife.

"Anna's upset, I suppose?"

"I don't know. Why should I be interested? Surely we've got more interesting things to talk about? When you've washed your hands there's an article in *The Economist* I want you to read."

As he washed Andrew sighed. Doris was upset and, from the sound of it, that film was the reason. All very well for Dad to tell him to talk about christenings to take her mind off it. Dad hadn't got to live with Doris. She was never sulky, but she frightened him when she flared up about nothing, and it meant she set him punishment tasks. He had been given articles to read in *The Economist* before. He knew it would be above his head, and she knew it too.

Emma prepared Dad-Tring's favourite supper. His slippers and paper were waiting as usual by the fire. She had her coat on, ready to walk round the garden with him, admire the bulbs and listen to his ideas on what would do well that summer. She had her reward: by the time supper was finished and the dishes washed he was at his most contented. He lay back in his chair smoking his pipe and smiling.

"Finished, Emma? Good! Come and sit down, old lady, there's that funny chap on the wireless in half an hour."

Emma sat and started to knit.

"I suppose you've heard this talk of Paul being thought of for a film."

Dad-Tring snorted.

"Sick of this film talk. Lot of nonsense. I shouldn't wonder if we've heard the last of it now, though. Ruthie won't want Paul mixed up in it; she's a different cup of tea from that silly Anna."

Emma's face showed nothing but interest. Her knitting-needles clicked cosily.

"That's right; but when I heard I thought to myself I bet Dad's having a laugh. He'll see the funny side of it being Peter, who works in the shop, whose boy has been picked, not high-and-mighty Anna's."

Dad thought this over and chuckled.

"I wouldn't be poor old George to-night. I expect he's goin' through the hoop."

"I suppose Peter is bound to set his face against Paul film-acting, but I expect you half wish he'd let the child do it. You're a sly one, but you can't fool me you wouldn't enjoy seeing Peter and Ruth being the ones to cause a bit of a flutter."

Dad brooded on this. Presently his face wrinkled, then he threw back his head and let out a roar.

"Properly put the cat amongst the chickens, that would—poor old Anna!"

"And poor Doris. It's natural, I suppose, seeing what Anna's accustomed to and Doris being so clever, but they're a bit lah-di-dah with Ruth, aren't they?"

"Let 'em be. Ruthie's worth six of either of 'em any day. I told Andrew if he had any nonsense with Doris ganging up with Anna over this he could take her mind off the subject by talking about getting her boys christened."

Emma did not stop knitting, but her mind worked quickly. It distressed her that her grandsons were not christened, but she believed Doris had a right to her point of view, however wrong to her that point of view might be. She did not believe Doris would change her views, but it might be that the christenings, or rather the absence of them, could be useful now in some way.

"I wonder . . ."

"Wonder what?"

"I was just thinking . . . Do you suppose, if you were to talk to Peter, if the chance came, he'd let Paul act in a film?"

Dad gaped at her.

"Let him! Have you gone mad, old dear? Whatever would I do that for?"

"You mentioning the christenings. You know how it is, a proper shake-up makes everybody behave differently to what they would do. Paul being a film actor would properly shake Anna and Doris up, wouldn't it?"

Dad's eyes twinkled.

"It would teach Mrs. 'Jist-Fency' something."

Emma smiled admiringly at him.

"Who's the clever old thing? I can see what you're planning. You're thinking, if it happened, you could seem to side with Anna, and that might be just what's wanted to get her off her high horse and settle down and become properly one of the family."

Dad was not one for worrying unduly. He did not think George and Andrew had picked well when they chose Anna and Doris; he didn't like the way they treated Emma, and they were not as much a part of his family as he could wish. No good worrying, he had told himself; they would settle in time. But they certainly were taking a long time about it, and somehow George and Andrew did not seem to be able to handle them right. Maybe if he took a hand, let Anna feel her father-in-law could back her up, it might help. He was pleased with himself. It was quite a smart idea. It might be that he could do something with Doris too. A big get-together with her and Anna might soften them both—make them nicer to Emma and easier to get on with. It would be worth a trial. This christening business was a damn disgrace, him being a sidesman and all; there was talk, and no wonder.

"Do you reckon there really is some chance for young Paul in a film?"

"I don't know, dear; but I'm sure there's been a letter. It won't be much, of course, a baby like that. Most like two or three days' work."

Dad made a face.

"I don't like to think of a grandson of mine . . ."

"Of course you don't, but, being the clever one you are, you'll see what's right; you always do. If there should be an offer, Paul's so small it couldn't hurt him, and maybe you'll decide that there'd be more good come out of it than harm. Turn on the wireless, dear; we don't want to miss that comic."

The Rose of England Film studios were a shock to Ruth. She had visualised a vast, imposing palace of a place. Instead the studio car turned in at some gates, and in front of them lay long, low, yellow-coloured buildings that looked like big Army huts. Mona Bun met them. Mona's heart was singing. What a wonderful day this must be for Mrs. Tring and little Paul, for all the world like a fairy tale; one minute just an ordinary little boy and his Mum, and the next, because by chance the camera-boys decided to film his school, walking into the Rose of England studios almost certain to come out with a contract. "Heigho, heigho, on the way to Romance we go."

Mona was more of a personage than she had been at the film offices. To-day she was representing Mr. Dragon, which almost, for the time being, gave her the status of Mr. Dragon.

"There you are, Mrs. Tring. And how's Paul to-day? We are going straight in to the studio. Mr. Water is waiting for you, and later they'll take some stills. If only the weather was better we needn't have brought you to the studio, the pictures could have been taken outside your house."

Ruth, her face trained in Mr. Sholtz's office, continued to smile, but her inside dropped as if she were in a lift which had gone down too quickly. What a terrible idea! She couldn't have kept that a secret; the whole street would have turned out to watch, and the news would have been all over the town in a minute. The very worst way for it to reach Peter.

"I wasn't sure what Paul ought to wear—he always wears little blouses and short pants. . . ."

"And very nice. Mr. Water will want him just as he is. We'll take him along and I'll introduce him, and while they get to know each other you and I will have a nice cup of coffee. I'm sure you could do with a cup; such a nasty, raw day."

For the first time since the film had been talked of Ruth was frightened. What was she letting Paul in for? This was the first inkling she had received of what a film contract might mean. Miss Bun had spoken so firmly, almost as if Paul did not belong to his mother any longer, but was the property of the studio. She did not know that Mona had been instructed to say what she had by Mr. Dragon.

"Get the mother out of the way. Give her some coffee. Noel will get a far better idea of the kid if he has him alone."

Ruth answered politely but firmly:

"I'd rather stay with Paul. He's so little he might be shy."

Paul, skipping ahead of them, heard this and turned round.

"I won't be shy. Will the man be there who turns that wheel thing?"

Ruth nodded and smiled vaguely, then lowered her voice.

"He saw the cameras when they came to the school. You never heard anything like the questions he asked. I daresay he wouldn't be shy, but he's excitable."

Mona patted Ruth's arm.

"He'll be all right. We shan't be far away. I'll tell one of the boys to stand by and fetch us at once if he seems nervous or upset. We'll be watching when he's photographed; it's just for his talk with Noel Water. Mr. Water is directing the picture, you know, and if he has Paul alone he'll tell very quickly if he's what he wants and if he can do anything with him."

Noel Water was a long, thin, clever-faced young man, the son of a parson, who had started life as a schoolmaster. A lucky meeting on a summer holiday had brought him in contact with Mr. Dragon, and after a period of learning and probation, he had become one of his assistant directors and, finally, his leading director. He could make a bad film, but never a dull one or one without interest. Amongst his gifts was great sensitivity. He could sense the feelings of those with whom he was in contact, often more clearly than the owner of the feelings. He sensed that Ruth was uneasy for her son. While Mona took off Paul's coat, gloves and beret he led her to a corner of the studio. "I want Paul alone for about twenty minutes. Would that worry you? I'm going to tell him a story and we'll act it together. I'm no earthly as an actor, so I'd get self-conscious if you and Mona were listening. I hope you'll be here though for the photographs. I've told them to photograph him from all angles. You must have some copies of those."

"You'll have me called if he gets shy or anything?"

"Of course, my dear." He raised his voice. "Mona dear, give Mrs. Tring some coffee; she's cold. Come here, Paul. I want to show you something exciting."

The studio had been used for shots of a film of which the exteriors had been made in Venice. Most of the scenery had been removed, but because it was wanted for some final shots, a gondola had been retained; it was floating in a large tank.

Paul was attracted to Noel Water. He wore grey flannel trousers, a yellow polo-jersey, an old tweed coat and a woolly scarf hanging round his neck. The child had never seen anyone dressed like that before. His father, grandfather and uncles and their friends wore dark suits except when they were gardening, and even then they never looked like this man. He was so favourably impressed that he was prepared for such a man to do exciting things, and now he was doing them. Who else kept a big boat floating in water in their house? He looked up at Noel, his eyes shining. "Could we get in?"

"You're going to get in. You're going on a journey."

"A real one?"

"No, a pretend one. It's to an island. You'll tell me the things you see as you go along, and when you get to the island I want you to get out of the boat looking very grand."

Paul raised his chin and strutted.

"Like this?"

"Just like that; then I want you to see me, and I'm going to say, 'Where have you been, Paul?'"

"And I'll say I've been miles an' miles, all round the world in a 'normous great steamer."

"And I shall interrupt and say: 'That isn't true. You haven't been anywhere, Paul. You've been here all the time.'"

The light died in Paul's eyes.

"Are you cross?"

"I'll only be pretending. I'll be pretending to be a cross old man who doesn't know what lovely places you can go to by pretending."

Paul's chin was up again.

"I'll pretend I'm a very rude boy, and I'll kick the old man."

"Not in this game. You see, you've come ashore feeling proud, a great traveller, and when a cross old man spoils your game you'll feel miserable, won't you, and that nothing is fun any more? Do you think you could be clever enough to pretend all that, and act it for me?"

"I like acting. I was a Lamb in 'Bo-peep' and a bell in 'Mary, Mary', and millions of other things in end of school 'tainment."

Noel lifted the child into the gondola.

"Good! Now you're off. My goodness! what's this? Is it a whale? It couldn't be a whale, could it? Tell me what you think it is."

*

Mona and Ruth made friends over their coffee. Time passed so quickly it was a surprise when Noel led Paul in.

"Here's your son, Mrs. Tring. Mona dear, take Paul to have an ice-cream. Is that all right with you, Mrs. Tring? When Paul comes back we'll get on with the stills."

Paul was enjoying himself. He was unaware what was different, but, with the perceptiveness of his age, he sensed he was important to Mr. Water. There had been no school that day, so there had been no howls of "Pauly, Pauly perambulator", but he had been bitterly hurt at an age when wounds, though they may appear to heal, seldom do. He had not known he had wounds, still less that feeling important was balm to them. He just knew he felt happy. He rushed to Ruth.

"Mum, that man has a boat in his house; it's in the middle of the floor in much more water than a bath."

Ruth was puzzled. Noel, seeing her expression, laughed and explained about the gondola.

"But you mustn't call me 'that man', Paul. You must call me Noel."

The moment they were alone he turned to Ruth.

"He'll be fine. We must see the stills, of course, but he's sure to photograph well. A very imaginative child with the most expressive face. I shall need him almost at once. Is that all right?"

Ruth had not expected things to move so fast. She had taken it for granted that days would elapse before she heard if Mr. Dragon was pleased with the photographs.

"At once! But Mr. Dragon said you'd be writing to Peter—my husband—and me first."

Noel sensed she felt rushed. He spoke soothingly.

"Quite true, but that's the business end. I'm only telling you my end. You and I will have to get together about things. Do you know anything about film-making?"

Ruth shook her head.

"Well, one of the important things is what we call continuity. That means that the way Paul looks for the first shot is the way he has to go on looking. His hair, for instance . . ."

Ruth flushed.

"I meant to explain about that. It needs cutting I know."

"That's just what it doesn't need." Noel walked up and down the dressing-room frowning. "A child like your Paul sets one thinking. You know originally we only showed young Jonathan aged about twelve. The book is about his whole life. He's a horrible type—a crook, a liar and, finally, a murderer. The author showed how he got that way. He had illusions of grandeur, starting when he was a lonely, over-imaginative kid. He was first caught stealing when he was about twelve. Nicholas Dram's son, Robert, plays him at that age, but the trouble started farther back."

He swung round to Ruth, but she could see he was speaking out loud rather than to her. "The audience have got to understand; he must be a lovable child, poor little devil! so when the end comes they must be thankful, not only because a horrible type is about to be extinguished, but for the man himself. You know, 'There but for the grace of God go I—' stuff."

Ruth waited to see if Noel had more to say, then she put in gently:

"About his hair. His father likes it short; he says he won't have him looking a sissy."

Noel snapped away from his thoughts.

"I knew the moment I saw you that you and I would get on together. I don't want his hair to his waist, but a shade longer than it is, and it will have to be kept that way until we've finished with him. You'll see to that, won't you?" Ruth saw that he didn't expect an answer; he just trusted her.

"How long would you need him?"

Once more Noel paced up and down.

"This will be a Nicholas Dram picture, which is what the public pay to see, but you can't go wrong with a child like Paul. Film stars will put up with almost anything except having a child or a dog walk off with the picture. I haven't worked things out yet, but I should guess I'd use him off and on for six or eight weeks. Does he know why he's here to-day?"

"No, only to be photographed. I shall have to persuade his father to let him act if you want him. Paul needs something like this, but I didn't see any reason why I should bring the question up with his father until I know if you wanted him, so I couldn't say much to Paul; at his age you can't stop them talking if they feel like it."

"How old is he?"

"Four and a half."

"Good. No nonsense about lessons. We'll be finished with him before he reaches school age. We must see the stills, but he'll be photogenic, so he'll play Jonathan. I had a hunch from the beginning, and I'm seldom wrong when I have a hunch. You must tell your husband the contract's as good as in the bag, and you must explain to Paul what's cooking. Take him to see a film, tell him what I do in picture-making, give him some idea of what's coming to him. When we start work he shall see the rushes. He'll soon get the hang of things." He started pacing again. "It's really a more important age than twelve. Those big, expressive eyes. You could get anything out of a kid like that if you handled him right." He came back to Ruth smiling at her as if she were an old friend. "It's exciting, isn't it? You bring that child into the studio and it's as if you'd put a match to my imagination." He took her arm. "Come on, we'll go and watch them take the stills."

CHAPTER 4
Emma Takes a Hand

Dad-Tring was not one as a rule to let things get on his mind. The moment he felt something irritating him he got annoyed, and then he took action. His unchristened grandchildren had been on his mind, and though he was annoyed, he had not taken action. This was partly due to Emma's tact but mainly to the doctor. Doctor Charles Wilks was the jovial, friend-of-the-family type of doctor. He had owned an enormous practice in which he had, with the quietest of consciences, soaked the rich to pay for the poor. With the coming of the National Health Service, still with the quietest of consciences, he had so balanced his affairs that he might live in the manner to which he was accustomed. The poor and medium incomes obviously paid nothing, but the rich, in spite of sticking expensive stamps weekly on to a health card, got no visits from him unless they paid, and paid in cash. "Must do it," he told Dad-Tring. "They can come to my surgery if they like, but if they want to lie in their beds it's cash; with those few pounds free of income tax I can just get by."

Dad-Tring knew this to be only a partial truth. He was quite aware that many guineas free of income tax slipped into the doctor's pockets, but he also knew that if there were real illness it made no difference whether the patient were rich or poor, the doctor would be at the bedside fighting for a life or easing somebody's way out of the world, with never a thought of himself, rewards from the Health Service or from anybody else. Dad thought the world of the doctor. They were fellow Masons and Rotarians, and were usually to be seen roaring with laughter while they told each other broad jokes; actually beneath this façade of merriment they were solid friends. The doctor shortened Dad-Tring to D.T., and Dad called him Charles. It had been in one of their quiet, friendly times together that the unchristened state of Jimmie had first been discussed. The doctor had listened while Dad, his face more like the cliffs of Dover than usual, had exploded about "That damn daughter-in-law of mine". "Never have anythin' to do with a clever woman, Charles," and "It's a disgrace that's what it is. A grandson of mine no better than a heathen." When there was a pause he had broken in:

"Nothing to do with me, of course, D.T., but I see a lot of women every day, and your Doris may be pig-headed, but she's not a fool. If she says she won't have little Jim christened, then she won't. That clever sort would rather be burned at the stake than do something that seems to them old-fashioned and foolish."

Dad had let out a sound as if he were ejecting Doris from his mouth.

"You call a christenin' old-fashioned or foolish?"

"I don't. I don't call curing a wart by as near as damn-it witchcraft, foolish or old-fashioned—in fact I believe in it—but if young Jim was all over warts I wouldn't suggest to Doris that she took him to a gipsy fortune-teller instead of to me; she'd think I belonged to the Middle Ages. Same with christenings; she believes making a cross on young Jim's forehead superstitious nonsense." He saw Dad was about to erupt again. "You take a word of advice, D.T., and, mind you, the vicar feels the same as I do; you won't do any good by forcing things. Christen a kid, take it to church every Sunday, teach it prayers, have it confirmed and more often than not by the time it's sixteen it's a heathen; but bring it up a heathen and you may have a devout churchman. I've seen that happen many a time, and so have you."

Dad had struggled to use the doctor's advice. Though sometimes it was almost beyond his powers, he had kept off the subject of christenings when Doris was present; but keeping off something which was constantly in the forefront of his mind was, he found, like rubbing an irritated spot. All very well for Charles and the vicar to say "Don't force things"; they hadn't got unchristened grandchildren; if they had he would bet there'd be no talk of "Don't force", it would be "Off to the font with them, and no nonsense."

His talk with Emma made Dad thoughtful, and the more he thought the better he liked the idea of putting a squib amongst his daughters-in-law. It tickled his sense of humour that he should kid Anna and Doris. He would like to see them making a fuss of him and Emma for a change, and there might be a lot to it; a shake-up could do wonders for people. The business would want careful handling; he couldn't talk to Peter himself—that would properly let the cat out of the bag. Charles must do it. When, the next morning, the doctor, as he often did, called in at Tring's for something, Dad was waiting for him. He took him into the back of the shop.

"Light your pipe, Charles; I want a word with you."

"This film business? Anything coming of that?"

"Peter hasn't said so, but I've been thinkin', suppose it did, if it mightn't be a good idea. Anna thought it was little Wendy was wanted. Wouldn't do her any harm to be taken down a peg, would it? Altogether too high and mighty. Then there's Doris; proper stirred up she'd be at Peter and Ruth's kid bein' made a fuss of. When there's a stirring-up you can get things done." Dad winked at the doctor. "I can't let on I'm in favour, you know; must let Anna and Doris think I'm as upset as they are."

The doctor lit a cigarette. From constant playing of humorous parts with the local amateurs and being considered a humorist at all times, his face was creased with lines of laughter, and soberness lay queerly on it; but Dad knew, as the sick knew, it looked very lovable when serious.

"You're an old fox. Still harping on those christenings." He was silent for a time. "Matter of fact, shouldn't wonder if there was something in this film business. I saw your Ruth and Paul in the main car park two days ago. They were getting into a damn great Daimler, and there was a chauffeur."

"Ruthie! Well! It isn't like her to be deceitful."

"Why deceitful? If I know Mrs. Peter, she wouldn't say anything to her husband before she had to. Wouldn't want to upset him."

"Upset him! I like that. Peter wouldn't let her go galli-vantin' off to a film studio, and she knows it."

"Now, don't get excited, D.T. I'll tell you something. If Mrs. Peter took Paul to a film studio she took him because she thought it was good for him. If she didn't think it was for his good, wild horses wouldn't have dragged her there. She's the devoted mother all right."

"Nonsense! How could it be good for him?"

"God knows. But mothers get funny ideas." The doctor paused for thought. "If this film business does turn up you'll have trouble, you know. Young women who think they've married beneath them will go on all right if noth-ing upsets the routine. But pick out the sister-in-law that doesn't think she's anybody special, and make her Queen of the May or some such damn silly thing, and you may have real trouble."

"Do Anna and Doris good, silly cats!"

The doctor shook his head at Dad.

"Psychology was never your long suit. Your Doris is a clever girl, and there's not much for her to sharpen her brains on in this place; but it isn't Mrs. Andrew you have to worry about, it's Mrs. George. If your Anna feels slighted—which she will—you can expect anything. She might even leave George."

"What!"

"I mean it. I've brought all your grandchildren into the world, and you get to know women at a time like that. All the same, I'm not saying a show-down mightn't be a good thing. If you and Mrs. Tring could make a friend of Anna over this business, you would be doing George and the three kids a bit of good."

"What about Doris?"

The doctor laughed.

"Those christenings! Let them rest for the minute. The question is how're you going to set about this? Peter'll need some talking round, won't he?"

"That's what I wanted to see you about. Would you have a word with him?"

"To say what?"

"That if the film business crops up it might be good for Paul, or somethin'. You know the way to do it. Get him on one side, let him think you're speakin' behind my back."

The doctor got up.

"You are a cunning old fox! Does Mrs. Tring know what you're planning?"

Dad nodded.

The doctor prodded him in the ribs.

"Couple of foxes. Still, I suppose I must give in to you. I'll drop in this afternoon and have a word with Peter— say I've come for a bit of butter off the ration that you promised me; and you see it's waiting for me; no reason why I shouldn't be an old fox too."

The doctor had a busy day; but by cutting his lunch-time short, he managed to squeeze time for Peter. He found him alone behind a counter, and talked jokingly about his little parcel before, with apparent casualness, mentioning the film.

"I hear there's a chance they may want to use young Paul in a film."

Peter grinned.

"So they tell me; but I've not heard about it, and I don't want to."

"Hasn't Mrs. Peter talked about it to you?"

"No. Not a word."

The doctor leant on the counter. He spoke quite sincerely, for he found it interesting that Ruth had not mentioned the film at all. He could quite understand that she would not want to argue the point until she knew there was something real to argue about; but there had been this letter sent to the school, which half the women in the place seemed to know about, and he would have thought she would have at least spoken of that.

"I suppose you'd be dead against letting him take a part if it was offered?"

Peter was amazed; he had always thought the doctor a man of wisdom.

"Of course. I wouldn't have a kid of mine mixed up in that world."

The doctor played with the string round his package of butter.

"May I give you a word of advice?" He did not wait for Peter's answer. "If this offer turns up, don't be in too great a hurry to turn it up." He looked over his shoulder in the direction of Dad-Tring. "I needn't ask you not to tell your father I've said this. It's between you and me."

Peter was utterly confused. What was the doctor driving at?

"Why?"

"Why indeed," thought the doctor. He found Peter's shocked blue eyes upsetting. It was like destroying the trust of a child; however, he comforted himself, this was not the first fairy tale he had invented for somebody's ultimate good. He was truly anxious about Anna; apart from his affection for Dad-Tring, he liked George, and he knew neither of them began to understand that there were such things as sick nerves, and that people could be really ill from them. "It would be just the thing for Mrs. Peter."

"Ruth! Why? What's the matter with Ruth?"

"Nothing, but a change is good for all of us. She's an American and she's settled down here well; but it must have taken a bit of doing. Strain, you know, adjusting yourself to a foreign country. If this business cropped up she'd be with the boy, see a new world and new faces. Make a great break for her, you know. Might be just what's needed."

Peter's expression changed.

"Oh! I never knew a change of people and things could do that trick."

The doctor thought fast. What on earth was the boy getting at? What trick? Suddenly he guessed. Well, no harm in his thinking that. Anything could do that trick, though with a good deal of accent on "could".

"It could. Of course, we don't know yet if the offer's coming, and it might be impossible—mean leaving home or something—but, as I say, all things being equal, if it turns up I'd think twice before turning it down."

"You bet I will, and so'll Ruth; why, even Dad would see the point of that."

The doctor put the package of butter in his pocket. It gave him a second to see how to get round that one.

"Ah, but you can't tell Mrs. Peter or anyone else; don't want her getting self-conscious and feeling all the family are looking at her—that would undo any good we might be doing. You'll have to find another excuse for giving your consent; and don't you worry what your family or anyone else says."

Peter's face was shining.

"You bet I won't! My back's broad. If only it works. We've been so browned off we've only got the one. I'd like a houseful of kids, and so would Ruth."

The doctor was going, but his conscience would not let him leave with that light on Peter's face.

"Don't count on it, old man; remember I said the operative word is *could*; this could do the trick, not *will* do it."

Peter nodded, but he was not bothering with any mights or buts. Nobody could be happier than he and Ruth; but it was queer they only had Paul. Made him wonder about himself, and he knew it upset Ruth. She didn't talk about it much, but there'd been a few days of hope sometimes, and he had seen her face when the hope died. He guessed that it was pretty often she had a tidy up of Paul's baby-things. If this film offer turned up, Ruth and all the family would think he was going off his rocker; but let them. Gosh! Suppose it was a girl. A little thing as pretty as Wendy but, of course, looking like Ruth. He had some orders to count; as he tossed packages into a box he whistled. Dad-Tring came across.

"You sound cheerful, son."

Peter smiled a secret smile.

"I am, Dad. Must be the spring."

Emma had woken up depressed. She was sure that Dad had taken on her plan, but how was he handling it? She kept looking at the clock. Ruth and Paul would be at the studio by now. Had Dad said anything to Peter yet? How soon was Anna to hear the news? Properly upsetting it all was, and all caused by a silly old film. She hoped she had done right in encouraging Ruth; not that it would have made any difference whether she had encouraged her or not. If only there had not to be all this deceit. Following a rule that had helped her all her life, she turned for help to work. The front room should have a real turn-out. Nothing like turning-out a room for keeping your mind off worries.

The room was only a quarter done when the gate clicked, and Emma saw Anna coming up the path. At no time did Emma care to be caught unawares by her daughters-in-law; for when she saw them she liked to be prepared in every way, but especially she disliked being caught at this moment by Anna, who, from the angle of her hat and a general dashed-out-all-anyhow look, seemed to be in a state.

Emma gave her overall a smooth-down, hurriedly untied the scarf that was over her hair, and attempted to seem normal. "Oh dear," she thought, "I'm sure she's heard something. If only I knew exactly what was happening. My goodness, I must be careful not to put my silly old feet in it."

Seen close to, Anna was definitely in a state. Her eyes were swollen, and she had forgotten to powder her nose or put on her lipstick. Emma said with determined naturalness:

"Good morning, dear. This is a nice surprise. Where are the children?"

Anna gave her an absent-minded peck on the cheek. "Iris is with them."

Not by the flicker of an eyelash did Emma show what she thought of that. She scorned George and Anna's Iris. She herself was helped on two mornings a week by a Mrs. Wintle. But Mrs. Wintle was a splendid housewife and a friend. Anna's Iris was a flighty, painted, curled, slovenly slip of a girl, whose only recommendation was that she was willing to dress up in a frilled apron and call herself a house-parlourmaid. It was very unlike Anna to trust her children to such a creature; in fact Emma never had heard of her doing so before. Anna felt Emma's surprise and disapproval.

"They'll be all right for this once. I simply had to see you. Have you heard anything?"

Emma was afraid her hands were trembling. She put them in her overall pockets.

"About what, dear? Come in the kitchen and I'll make you a cup of tea."

Anna followed Emma into the kitchen. Once there, she plumped down into a chair by the table, tears rolling down her cheeks.

"I knew something was going on—you should have seen her—I'd taken the children out while I did the shopping—getting some socks for Wendy at Littleton's, the sock counter looks over the car park—there was an enormous car and a chauffeur! He held the door open for Ruth as if she were royalty—and then lifted Paul into the seat beside him . . ."

Emma was glad that filling the kettle made an excuse for keeping her back to Anna.

"A car and a chauffeur! Well, I never!"

Anna sobbed more loudly. "I won't stand it—it isn't fair—stuck here year after year in this miserable little town—knowing nobody—treated like dirt—wouldn't have minded so much, but it was almost a promise—everybody knew about it, Wendy ought to be in films—everybody has always said so—I can't think why any film company should look at Paul—he's spoilt to death as it is."

Emma fumbled for something to say.

"You don't know that they are going to use him, do you?"

"They're testing him, anyway—what else would Ruth be doing with a car and a chauffeur? Don't suppose she's ever spoken to a chauffeur before—silly, common little cat. . ."

Emma could not let that pass.

"That won't do, Anna. I know you're upset, but that's no way to talk about Ruth, and you know it. You have a cup of tea and you'll feel better. Suppose Paul is given a little part in a film; you mustn't let it upset you like this."

Anna's head shot up.

"You think he may get a part—I believe you know something—but you're not going to tell me Dad-Tring would let him take it—or Peter either, if it comes to that."

Emma fetched two cups and put them on the table. The movement gave her time to think and see what reply she should make.

"You're right about that. If it happens, you're likely to hear Dad-Tring say a lot of things he shouldn't."

Anna beat on the table with her fists.

"It mustn't happen—it mustn't—it mustn't!"

Emma looked at the girl anxiously.

"It's no good shouting, dear. I'll never tell anyone I hold with film-acting for children—I don't—but it's foolish for us to get upset if it happens. This is Ruth and Peter's business . . ."

"It ought to be stopped by law—he's a horrible, spoilt child—it'll ruin him . . ."

"Maybe, but it's not a thing we can interfere in. We can try and dissuade them if we think it right . . ."

"Right! Dad-Tring ought to refuse to let Peter work for him any more—he ought . . ."

Emma had made the tea. She put a cup down by Anna. "Anna dear, you and I don't belong to the same class, and that gives us different ways of thinking; but I do know one thing which is true in all classes. Being jealous is terrible; it only hurts the jealous one. If this should happen why don't you put a proud face on it? Pretend to everybody that you don't care . . ."

"But I do care—I was going mad in this place as it was—everybody so snooty—you won't understand what this chance for Wendy meant—no more looking down their noses—new people to meet—the fun of it all—now Ruth's to have it—everybody laughing behind my back—why should Ruth have it? She's happy as it is—she never knew anything better—she thinks everybody here grand—I can't stand it, I tell you—if Ruth is to have everything—I'll kill myself. . ."

Emma knew nothing of frustration, how watching others being big fishes in a little suburban pond could hurt a girl like Anna. She had always been satisfied with her place in society and proud to be Dad's wife. But she had the imagination to grasp that Anna had reached breaking point, and she knew she had neither the words nor the wisdom to help the girl. She did the only thing she felt it right to do: she stroked Anna's hair and spoke as she would have done to a child.

"There, love—there, don't cry. There's a way round everything. You come up to my bed and lie down." Anna moved as if to throw her hand off. "Now you listen to me, dearie. You can't go running about the street with your pretty face looking like that. I'm going to tuck you up on my bed with a hot-water bottle."

Anna could scarcely speak.

"The children—I've got to give them their lunch—Iris . . ."

"That's all right, dearie. As soon as I've got you tucked up warm I'll pop round and see to the children. I'll bring them all here for the afternoon . . ."

Emma tidied her face and hair and put on her hat. On her way out she paused at her front room; it was terrible to leave it like that; whatever would anyone think? Still, no good troubling about that now; she must think of Anna. Maybe after a sleep, when she heard the children playing in the garden and knew that Caroline was outside in her pram, she would fancy a bit of dinner. Just as she was leaving the house a thought struck her. It would be a nice thing if Ruth telephoned while she was out! She easily might. It would properly blow things up if Ruth telephoned and it woke Anna up and she answered it. She lifted the receiver and replaced it crookedly. It wouldn't ring that way, and if Anna should notice it, then it would only seem like carelessness.

Doris opened Anna's door to Emma. Both women, though they hid it well, were dismayed at the sight of the other. Doris was already furious with herself that she had let her curiosity get the better of her. She had not intended to. She had started out for a walk with the children with no idea of visiting Anna, but somehow on the way home she had found herself saying, "Funny we haven't run into Anna. Wonder if she's ill? I suppose it would be kind to just ask." Though in her secret heart she knew she was making excuses, she had not been able to resist the urge to open Anna's gate. Once inside the house there had been no chance to withdraw. Iris was in a hopeless muddle. Silly, slovenly little thing she might be, but, as the eldest of a family of six, she was used to coping with children and delighted to do it. When Doris arrived she had forgotten she was a house-parlourmaid and had become a bandit, Wendy assisting as a gangster's moll, both busy kidnapping John: Geoffrey was the hero detective. Iris, rapt in the game, was oblivious of the appalling smell of a burning saucepan, which she had left on the stove, the knocking of the baker to ask about bread, or the gas-man shouting to be let in to read the meter. Doris took charge. She did not like bribing children, but she promised ice-cream if Geoffrey would invent a nice, quiet game to amuse himself, Wendy and Jimmie. For safety she put Caroline's pram beside John's on the front path. She discovered how much bread was wanted, soothed the gas man, removed the debris of the saucepan to the dustbin, then sat down to cross-examine Iris.

Iris's story was not lacking in imagination. However, her description of Anna's return from the shopping expedition, even if only a quarter true, made it clear to Doris that Anna had heard or seen something to upset her.

"Created alarmin' she did, Mrs. Andrew. White as a sheet she was. 'Er 'at on one side of 'er 'ead, and 'er eyes wild like you see in the photos of them murderers. 'You do look queer,' I says, but she was past 'earing; she jus' gives the children a push. 'Look after them, Iris,' she says, and then she's out of the 'ouse an' runnin' down the road like a copper was after 'er."

"Didn't she say where she was going?"

"Not a word." Iris's voice took a sinister note. "Do you know what I think? She's thrown 'erself in the river."

"Don't be silly, Iris. There isn't a river."

Iris was not put off by a little thing like the absence of water.

"Under a train, then. My Dad's a chimney-sweep, and he's seen some funny things in 'is time. 'E says when they want to do it, they does it."

Doris questioned the children.

"Do you know where your mother's gone?"

Geoffrey was busy marrying Wendy to Jimmie. "And then you say 'I will,' Jimmie, and Wendy, you say, 'I don't mind if I do.'" He broke off impatiently to answer Doris. "You're interrupting a wedding. Mummy didn't say where she was going."

Wendy skipped over to her aunt.

"I think she was going to be sick. Her mouth was shut like holding sumptin' back."

Geoffrey caught hold of Wendy.

"You can't walk away like that, in the middle of your wedding; brides don't. Can I fetch John, Aunt Doris? We want him for the baby they have at the end of me marrying them."

In the ordinary way Doris would have answered that, for Jimmie was brought up on the facts of life, but to-day she had to let it pass.

"Do you think your mother was ill, Geoffrey?"

"Her face was yellow and blue and striped when we came out of Littleton's."

Doris went back into the house. She sent Iris out for the ice-creams, and started to prepare lunch. She knew it was idiotic, but she felt nervous. Suppose Anna came back and found her not only messing about in her kitchen, but that she had sent her so-called house-parlourmaid out on a message. It would be no good explaining how good her intentions were, that no woman could possibly not have stayed to help; if Anna were in the state it seemed she was in, she would be past listening to what was said, and would fly off the handle at anything. If only she had not come round this morning she would not have known anything was wrong, and so would not have got mixed up in the fuss. Even now, with any luck, she would have prepared the children's lunch and left it for Iris to give them—surely that little idiot could manage that—and would be home before Anna came back. It was at that moment in her reasoning that she heard the gate click. Certain it was Anna, and not wishing to be caught in her kitchen, she ran to open the front door, and so found herself face to face with Emma.

"Doris! Anna didn't say you were here."

"What's the matter with her?"

Emma was not answering that right away. Anna and Doris were supposed to be friendly, but it had been to her Anna had come in her trouble, not to Doris.

"Where are the children?"

Doris explained about the game and that she had sent Iris for ice-cream.

"I had no idea Anna wasn't here. I came round about something, and found a saucepan burning in the kitchen and bells ringing while that little fool Iris played some game with the children with a lot of screaming in it. I don't know what Anna would have said; you know what she is about the neighbours and noise."

Emma walked down the passage to the kitchen. She looked round approvingly. Doris might be the clever one, but she was practical. She had found what was for dinner and was preparing it nicely. Through the window she could see the three children playing happily and reasonably quietly. At that moment she liked Doris better than she had since Andrew first brought her to see her.

"What can I do?"

"There's some more vegetables to prepare; Anna had planned a stew. There's an apron on that door. What's up with Anna? Iris says, and so do the children, that something upset her at Littleton's."

Emma tied on the apron and went to the sink to wash some carrots.

"She certainly isn't well. I've put her to lie down on my bed."

"Cagey old thing!" thought Doris. "Well, I suppose one of us has got to say what we know, and it looks as if it will have to be me."

"She's been upset about Paul getting a film test instead of Wendy. Was it to do with that?"

"Yes. You know how you can see the car park from some of Littleton's windows. She says she saw Ruth and Paul get into a big car. She said there was a chauffeur."

In a flash Doris saw that scene. Anna out shopping, pushing a pram, keeping an eye on Geoffrey and Wendy, then that view of Ruth and Paul, the quintessence of all she had hoped for herself and Wendy. For once she was not being clever, or thinking she knew all the answers; she said sincerely the first thing that came to her mind.

"Must have sent her crackers."

Emma was humbled. How clever Doris was! She evidently understood Anna.

"That's not the way I'd have put it, dear; but it's somewhere near the truth." She turned. "I'm worried, Doris. Anna was quite hysterical. I didn't know how to help her. It seems to me so silly—not a thing that a sensible girl could really mind about to that extent."

Had Doris been able to blush she would have blushed. The obvious bewilderment in Emma's voice made her ashamed. It was silly, and she had not been so far from sharing that silliness herself. Well, this would be the end of it. She would put pettiness and jealousy out of mind. Mum-Tring, who was a hopeless reactionary, muddle-headed, smugly and happily lower middle-class, ought not to be able to make someone of her education and with her brains feel ashamed.

"What did you say to her?"

Emma was not going to tell Doris of such nonsense as "I'll kill myself" or the shocking way Anna had spoken of Ruth.

"There was nothing much I could say; she was in no state to listen—I tried to soothe her, and I got her to lie down and gave her a hot-water bottle, and two aspirins. I hope she's asleep."

"I wonder if Paul is going to get a part in a film. If he does Anna might do anything, you know—it's not only the film . . ."

Emma made tch-tching sounds. It was shocking to hear her worst fears put into words. Poor George! His home must be kept together. For a wild moment Emma examined the idea of running round to Ruth's house and waiting until she came in, and then pleading with her.

Then in her memory she saw Ruth's expression as she said, "I'm not afraid of being unpopular with the family if what I am doing is right for Paul." There was no help to be had there; to everyone else it might seem nonsense, but Ruth believed film-acting would be good for Paul, and she would fight for what she thought good for her child. She could not bring herself to discuss George and Anna's life with Doris. Every instinct she had screamed at her that discussing the private affairs of one child with another, however urgent the need to understand, was wrong. Nor, even had she been able to talk, was this the moment; there were plans to be made. She brought the washed and sliced carrots to the table.

"There, that isn't much help; but I think I'll have to be going. Don't want Anna to wake and feel she's got to rush round here. Had you planned to stay?"

Doris explained that she was hoping Iris could cope once the meal was on the stove. Emma looked doubtful.

"If I took Wendy and Caroline, could you stay here? With just you, Iris, the two boys and baby John there'd be enough."

Doris nodded.

"Lovely of you, dear. I'll bring Wendy and Caroline in then. I'll dress them up prettily. Anna will like that."

Half an hour later Doris stood at Anna's gate. She watched Emma pushing Caroline's perambulator down the path, and the way she smiled at Wendy, who danced beside it. It was clever of the old thing to have thought of dressing them up in their best things. It was wise of her to understand that Anna needed coping with. It had been she who remembered ice-cream had been promised, and said she would buy some for the little girls on her way home. It was a depressing thought, because it was against everything that she believed, but it did seem that even reactionary types had their moments of vision.

The photographing took far longer than Ruth had allowed for. Every angle of Paul's face was studied, and so were the positions which came natural to him. Every few minutes Noel said in a sharp whisper, "And that one," or "Can you catch that?" When the photographing was over it was lunch-time, and it was taken for granted that they would stay. Mona came to the fore again.

"I'll show you where you can wash, Mrs. Tring, and then we'll go to the canteen. I told them about Paul. They have some chicken for him. Will that be all right?"

Paul was always a slow eater, but in the canteen he continually forgot to eat. The company were making a musical about Elizabethan England, and on that day they were using over a hundred extras. As well some of those concerned in the final shots of the Venice film were at the next table. Two clowns in spangled satin suits, white socks and felt hats were at a table in Paul's line of vision. He had no idea where he was, and was not really surprised at what he saw. He believed that Father Christmas filled his stocking from a sleigh pulled by reindeer, and it was only because he came in the middle of the night that he had not seen him. He did not question that all the nursery rhyme and fairy-tale characters were alive, though not exactly as alive as he was. He knew that angels guarded him and that he might see one any day. He took the canteen to be Noel Water's dining-room, so that his fellow-guests should be so unusual and exciting was satisfying; it killed hints that had reached him at school about what was real and what was pretence. When at last he had finished his lunch and Mona and Ruth were leading him out, and they came upon one of the studio cats, it was in all sincerity that he remarked:

"I suppose he talks jus' as well as us."

Ruth was sorry at this backsliding, and answered gravely:

"That's a silly way to speak, Paul dear. You know cats don't talk."

Mona said:

"That's Blackie. There's a lot of those black cats around; I expect there's some kitties somewhere—the old stork brings lots of kitties to the studios."

Paul gazed up at her.

"What's a stork?"

"A big white bird, dear."

Paul did not answer, and Ruth and Mona talked to each other across him. Mona had been instructed to show them round, and she did it thoroughly. As they walked up one vast passage and down the next, pausing at doors while words like "Wardrobe" and "Make-up" floated over him, Paul gazed anxiously round, Mona's words spinning in his head. "A big white bird." He mustn't miss so gorgeous a sight. A big white bird carrying kittens. Miss Bun had said the bird brought lots. No big white bird ever carried kittens to his home; it was only Noel Water's house that white birds carried kittens to, and that boats floated in water in. He was absorbed searching for the bird, and so certain he would see it that it was a shock to hear Ruth tell him they were going home, and he was to say goodbye.

He was tired and had been mentally excited by Noel; in a fury he flung himself at Ruth.

"I won't go home, I won't—not till I seen the big white bird."

Ruth was upset. She had hoped for signs that Paul's compensating was beginning.

"That's very naughty, Paul. You have surely had a wonderful day, and this is not a nice way to behave."

At Paul's first scream Mona became entirely Mr. Dragon's secretary. Mr. Dragon was pleased he had discovered this little boy, and Mr. Dragon must not be upset, which he certainly would be if he heard the child had screamed and made a scene at the studio. She smiled blandly, as if Paul were behaving beautifully, while she beckoned to the chauffeur.

"Take him to sit beside you, Smithson." Ruth held out a hand to stop Smithson, who did not like children to scream, and would clearly tell Paul so when he had him on his own; but Mona prevented her. "You leave him to Smithson. Mr. Dragon would wish it."

"But he might hold his breath."

Mona looked dismayed.

"I hope not. Mr. Dragon would not like to hear of that." Mr. Dragon! Once more Ruth felt afraid. Why should it matter what Mr. Dragon liked? It was her Paul that mattered. She managed, as she got into the car, to smile and wave to Mona, but she felt worried. But soon she was relaxed; Paul was not holding his breath, he had not screamed since Smithson had picked him up. She let her mind drift from Paul to Peter. She had to speak to him tonight. She would telephone Mum-Tring; perhaps she would advise her of the best mode of approach.

"At that house we was in," Paul told Smithson, "there was a 'normous bird what brings kittens, Miss Bun told me so, but it didn't come to-day."

"Nor it wouldn't," said Smithson. "Never of a Thursday."

When Emma arrived with the children, Anna was awake. As she opened the front door Emma gave an anxious look at the telephone. Thank goodness it had not been touched. It was lucky she had thought of it; it made her shiver to think what Ruth might have said if she had spoken to Anna without realising who it was. Anna would have been sure to think she was being deceitful, which in a way she supposed she was, only it was meant to be good deceit if there could be such a thing. It was not only pity, but a guilty conscience which warmed her voice as she spoke to Anna.

"Well, dearie, so you are awake. Look who's here to give their Mummie a kiss."

The sleep had given Anna some measure of control, and she was able to feel pleasure in her children's appearance.

"Grannie has been dressing you up. Where's Geoffrey?"

Emma explained in part what had happened. She did not mention Iris, and managed by slurring her story to give the impression that she and Doris had arrived at the house more or less simultaneously.

"I told her you had come to see me and I had made you lie down as you looked so poorly, and she suggested seeing to the boys, and I said I'd look after the little girls. I hope I've done right, dear."

Anna was exhausted. She was glad to be planned for and looked after. She knew it was only a breathing space, as if she had run for a moment behind a wall to get out of the wind; but the wind was still tearing and roaring outside, and she would have to battle with it again, but she needed the rest. If Mum-Tring would give the children lunch and she could be here a bit longer her strength would come back—strength to fight—and she would have a chance to plan. If Ruth had a film offer for Paul, and she and Peter accepted it, what should she do? She was not going on as she was; that was a certainty. She would die rather than remain the small-town wife, with people sniggering behind her back because Ruth had got the chance she wanted. As these thoughts chased each other through her head, her colour rose. Emma looked at her anxiously.

"Now do relax, dearie. Would you like the children with you while I get their dinner?"

Anna closed her eyes.

"Would you mind? I want to be alone."

"Of course, dear; and presently I'll bring you up a little something to eat. Come on, Wendy. You and Caroline and I will have dinner together. Won't that be fun?"

As the door closed Anna opened her eyes. "Won't that be fun! Poor old idiot!" She probably thought that after a sleep, an aspirin, and a cup of tea everything would blow over. Well, she had another think coming.

Dad-Tring had an inward glowing. He had done that all right. He had no idea what the doctor had said to Peter, but it must have been the right thing, for Peter looked pleased, and twice he had caught him whistling. Comic he should be wishing for that film offer to turn up for Peter, seeing how he disliked the idea; still, if it got Jimmie and John to the font, it was worth it. Now, he supposed, he ought to start palling up with Andrew, to get ready for the row with Peter and Ruth if it came. Andrew must be able to report to Doris that the old man would be flaming mad if it happened.

"Care for a drink on the way home, Andrew old man?" Andrew was surprised and showed it. Dad had a drink every evening at "The Green Man", where he met the doctor and other cronies of his, for the saloon bar of "The Green Man" was really a club. It was never stated that you could only drink in the saloon bar of "The Green Man" between opening time and seven by invitation of the landlord; but, nevertheless, it was a local, unwritten rule. He and George and Peter had all been taken there for drinks, but usually for some reason. George had been several times when he was demobbed, and he and George had been brought there to receive congratulations on their engagements, and Peter on his marriage. There were drinks there on birthdays and public occasions—Christmas and so on—but to-day was, as far as Andrew knew, any old Thursday. However, an invitation to go to "The Green Man" was a command. He grinned and nodded.

Charles Wilks had called in at "The Green Man" especially to have a word with Dad, and he did not allow the presence of Andrew to interfere with that. He beckoned Dad into a corner and held him by the lapel of his coat, as he did when he wanted to whisper an especially juicy story, while he told him of his talk with Peter. If anyone had doubted it was a story which the two friends were sharing it was dispelled by Dad's behaviour. He threw back his head and an enormous laugh rumbled up from the pit of his stomach. Each time the laugh died away he re-thought of what Charles had said, and it started him off again. Between laughs he gulped, "If that doesn't beat cock-fighting." "If you want another baby put your children to work in films." When at last his laughter died he remembered Andrew. Wiping his eyes, he turned Charles so that his back was to the room.

"I brought Andrew along. I want to say something to show him whose side I'll be on if the balloon goes up. Got any ideas?"

Charles thought for a moment.

"Yes. Tell him what I told you about seeing Ruth and Paul get into that car." He dug Dad in the ribs. "I'm telling you about it now. Get your heavy-father expression ready. Let Andrew see you're upset."

Dad drew his mouth down and frowned. Before he turned he gave Charles a broad wink.

Doris had just put Jimmie to bed when Andrew came in.

"Hullo. What kept you?"

"Dad. He took me to have a drink at 'The Green Man'. The doctor was there; he told the old man something that made him in a state. I don't know when I saw him so angry. Funny business, the doctor was passing the car park and . . ."

Doris stopped him.

"Don't tell me. He saw Ruth and Paul get into a large chauffeur-driven car."

"Yes, a Daimler. How did you know?"

Doris put her arm through his.

"Come and look at the garden. This has been quite a day."

While he peered at seedlings, Andrew heard all that had happened.

"She can't really mind all that much, can she?" he asked. "I mean, she'll get over it."

Doris shrugged her shoulders.

"I was still at her house when she came back. She didn't say much, but she looked awful. She did say your mother had been good, which she was. I've a suspicion your mother, without understanding what it's all about, has arrived at what it might add up to for George."

"What could it add up to?"

Doris shrugged her shoulders.

"My guess is as good as another's, but it's only a guess, and I'm not saying what it is. You just think about Anna, the type she is, the way she feels about this place and George and your family, and you'll get an idea what she felt like when she thought she was going to rise in a blaze of glory, and what she'll feel like if Ruth gets the glory instead of her."

"Lot of nonsense! She might be a bit browned off but, after all, what is a small film part, anyway?"

The moment he had spoken Andrew looked anxiously at Doris. That was the kind of statement that usually got her goat. But Doris, though she appeared amused, remained tranquil.

"We'll see. I'm glad it's nothing to do with us. If this film happens—and I must say with this story of cars it sounds likely—we must somehow manage to remain neutrals."

"Not so easy, old girl. You ought to have heard Dad. It's funny, you know; it isn't like Ruth, somehow, sneaking off like that. Anyway, I shouldn't think it will happen; Peter won't have it."

Doris laughed.

"Oh? As I said just now, we'll see."

Andrew accepted that. He was grateful that something had made Doris so unusually tolerant. Almost like the Doris he had met at the summer school. If only she was more often like this he would be a better companion for her. He wasn't really stupid; at school they had thought him quick. But she scared him with her sharp answers.

Ruth was bathing Paul when Peter came home. She was tired and a little nervous. Things had moved so fast— so much faster than she had intended. It had upset her to be unable to telephone. The telephone girl said the receiver had not been put down properly all afternoon but now it was right, but there was no answer. It was kind of upsetting that Emma was out. She had pictured her waiting for her to call her up. She would have been glad not only of her advice, but of her support. She would have liked to have gone round to see her, but it had already been a long day for Paul. Through the steam of the hot water she smiled at Peter.

"Here it comes," she thought; "Paul's bound to talk about the studio."

Peter looked at Ruth. How lovely she was! She looked so right stooping over Paul. It was all wrong they only had the one child. He spoke from a full heart.

"Darling, did you take Paul to a film studio?"

Ruth straightened up, and tried to gather her courage for what she must say.

Paul beamed at his father.

"At Noel's house where we was there was a boat in water. I wish we could keep a boat in our house."

Peter sat on the edge of the bath.

"Do you, old man?" He turned to Ruth. "What's it all about? Do they really want him?"

Ruth, though her hands trembled, answered with apparent calm.

"I think so. It's the film of a book called *Cast a Stone*. I've got the book, if you'd like to read it. The Rose of England Company, which has a Mr. Dragon as chief, is making the picture of the book. Nicholas Dram plays the lead called Jonathan; a man called Noel Water is directing the picture; I never heard of him, though I guess Mr. Dragon thought I should have. In the film there are scenes that go way back to Jonathan's childhood. Most of the scenes are acted by Mr. Dram's son, who is around twelve, I think; but Mr. Dragon and Mr. Water figured that there should be scenes of him as a little boy . . ."

"And they want Paul?"

"Yes, I guess so. I didn't know things would move that fast. I figured it would be weeks before anyone made a decision, but right from the start—that was the day before yesterday when we saw Mr. Dragon and to-day when we went to the studio to let them photograph Paul and meet Mr. Water—it seemed everything was kind of fixed."

Paul had various celluloid toys in his bath. He gave a fish a push.

"Look, Dad, he's going to bite you. You shouldn't call the gent'num Mr. Water, Mum; he said I was to call him Noel."

Neither Peter nor Ruth paid attention to this. Ruth said: "You mustn't think I was fixing things behind your back—I couldn't, anyway: you would have to sign—but there didn't seem any reason to trouble you until we knew . . ." The lameness of her excuses silenced Ruth. She looked miserably at Peter. She had to make him agree; she could not weaken over that. Her friend, the author of *The Mind and the Child* had made Paul's needs sufficiently clear to give her strength, but trying to explain why she had kept everything to herself was difficult going. She made another effort. "I knew this was important . . ."

Peter felt his heart contract with love for her; so she had the same idea as the doctor. Poor little Ruth! She had been so good; even now she wouldn't say right out what was in her mind, for fear of seeming to suggest there was anything missing for complete happiness.

"It's all right, darling. There's no need to explain. I think it just as important as you do."

Ruth gaped at him, tears of relief in her eyes.

"You do? Well. . . why, Peter . . ."

Peter felt the situation was getting out of hand. A bit off for parents to get emotional in front of the child; Mum and Dad had never done that. He seized the flannel Ruth was holding.

"Come on, young Paul. I'm going to scrub you. If you're going to act in a film, you must be clean."

Ruth watched father and son. The relief of not only having talked of the film to Peter, but finding that he agreed with her was too much. She had a lump in her throat; she longed to have a good howl. When she had control of herself, curiosity seized her. Why did Peter think the film important? He had thought it a horrible idea when it concerned Wendy. Surely she had not left the book about, and yet it did seem that he must have read it.

It was not until she and Peter had finished supper that she questioned him. Over supper she had found him curiously uninterested in the studio world. He seemed to place it, and their visit there, at about the same interest level as their going to a dentist—necessary but not worth talking about. Well, she reasoned, maybe that was as well. She could not see Peter fitting in with Noel Water. She could see him getting annoyed if he had to know that Mona Bun thought Mr. Dragon could decide what was right for his son. After all, that he agreed was all that signified. But why did he? It wasn't natural, some way. As she got up to clear the table she asked casually:

"Have you read *The Mind and the Child*?"

"No. I'll look through it, though. I ought to know what the story's about, I suppose; but I thought you said it was called *Throw a Stone*."

Ruth, utterly bewildered, fetched *Cast a Stone*.

As she went to and fro clearing the table she gave puzzled looks at Peter turning the pages of the book. He hadn't read *The Mind and the Child*. He hadn't even bothered to take in the name of the picture. He wasn't really interested in the picture. Then why did he say it was important? It was no surprise when she had finished washing up to find *Cast a Stone* on the floor, and Peter asleep.

No sooner had Anna and the children left for home than Emma, though her partially-turned-out front room screamed to be finished, put on her hat and coat and, carrying with care her string bag, went to George's office.

It was always queer to Emma to see George's name on a plate. She seldom visited his office, but each time she did it surprised her afresh. It was funny, he had been a grown man for years, and she thought of him as such, but when she saw that plate it pulled her up and made her smile. Her little George a solicitor!

George was looking through tomorrow's work. His typist, though officially it was not time to leave, was getting her face ready for an evening out with her boy friend. George was doing quite nicely; his father's friends put any work they could in his way, but no one could describe him as overworked. He was glad to see Emma; it was an excuse for finishing for the day. He told the typist she could get off as soon as she liked, and sat Emma in the clients' chair.

"This is nice, Mum. What's brought you along? Been picked up drunk?"

Emma put her string bag on the floor by her. She pretended to laugh at the little joke, but she did not feel like laughing. George wasn't looking well—sort of thin and harassed, too old for his age.

"I wanted a talk with you—just ourselves, what you used to call when you were little a bath-talk. Do you remember how you used to come into the kitchen and whisper 'Could we have a bath-talk to-night, Mum?' Only at that age you couldn't say 'bath', you always said 'barf'."

"Little scrounger, I was. It was always something I wanted, I bet."

Emma had her memories. She shook her head. "Not always. You look tired, George."

George lit a cigarette.

"I am. I don't know why, I haven't been pushed lately. I'm planning a holiday. I had thought of a farm somewhere—take the whole family . . ."

His voice trailed off. Because it was the wrong time of year for the sort of things he wanted to do, and he had not yet heard of the right place, his first rapture at the thought of Devon—glorious Devon—had died down. He did not want the bother of arranging to go to a farm miles from anywhere; he wanted to be able to say "Abracadabra" and find himself there.

George was not looking at Emma; had he been he would have seen the same half-amused, half-despairing twinkle in her eyes that was often there when she talked to his father. George was a proper Tring all right, she thought. A farm miles from anywhere with Anna. Bless the boy! What would he think of next?

"That would be very nice, dear; but I suppose, in your sensible way, you are wondering if you wouldn't do better to put it off until later in the year. I think that's wise of you. Might get any weather this time of year, even snow. All the same, I think you should plan a little break. What other ideas have you got in that clever old head?" George was always easy with his mother, and to-day she seemed especially soothing. The thoughts turning in his brain began to slip out.

"It's not so much a holiday I want—seem sort of fed-up generally—I suppose it's the same for everybody—hard to settle down—I know the war's been over for a long time but it still seems hard . . ."

"Must be. I think it's wonderful the way you have settled, and doing so well too . . ."

"Not badly, but it's mostly boring stuff."

"I suppose it is—wills and all that—but there's an interesting side to it too; I hear you've done a lot to help the Soldiers', Sailors' and Airmen's Families Association, and that."

"A bit. As a matter of fact I rather like lending a hand there. You see, a lot of the cases are the sort of thing I came up against in the Army; I know the types."

Emma caught a wistful note in his voice.

"Pity there are none of the officers you were with living near here."

George thought of his brother officers, and inwardly shuddered. He couldn't picture them in his home. He could imagine how they would come once and never again, driven out by butter-knives, doilies and refined conversation.

"Thank God there aren't. It's different now—we wouldn't get on."

Emma knew what he meant. She couldn't imagine men who were men liking all the nonsense that went on in Anna's home; not enough to eat and too many fancy things to eat with, and that flighty little Iris, with her dirty hands and frilled apron, and poor Anna with her BBC accent.

"It would be nice, though, if you had some friends near here. After all that time away, with the excitement and all, and nothing but men round you, I expect you find this rather a small place, full of silly women like me."

George's head shot up.

"If they were all like you, Mum. I expect it's my fault, but I can't live up to Anna."

Emma had hoped to hear a portion of the truth, but put bluntly like that George's words frightened her. However, she was here to help, not to consider her own feelings.

"Faults in married life are usually six of one and half a dozen of the other. Anna's a nice, pretty girl; but perhaps not the wife you would choose now, and I daresay you're not the husband she'd choose now. It's natural mistakes are made in a war. It's the feeling of rush, I expect. Besides, you don't see each other properly, not in your ordinary home and all that."

George nodded.

"Too true. It must be the spring—I've been properly fed up lately."

Emma felt the moment had arrived for which the visit was planned.

"I don't think it's only the spring, dear. I think Anna's been restless and unhappy for some time, and now something's turned up to make things worse."

She watched George's face before venturing to describe what had happened in his home and what Anna had said.

George listened to her in silence. When she had finished, he thought over what she had told him.

"If that's how she feels she'd better go."

Emma could have shaken him.

"You don't mean that. What would you do with three children, for I know you wouldn't let her have them?"

"Damned if I would."

"Of course not; nor, mind you, does Anna mean half of what she said. She thinks she does but not really. She wouldn't do anything to upset the children; she's a very good mother." George moved, and she smiled at him. "Perhaps I wouldn't bring them up the way she does, but she's a good mother all the same, and they're children to be proud of. No, what you have to do is to put your thinking-cap on. I needn't tell you that what you've got to find is more outside interests; you know that for your-self, and, being the clever old thing you are, at the same time you'll find something that will take Anna out more."

"Easier said than done."

"Not a bit of it. You've got in a rut, and want shaking out of it. You have a talk with Dad. If Paul acts in a film he'll need taking out of himself too; not the sort of thing he'd hold with, as well you know."

Emma got up. She kissed George. Then she opened the string bag, took out a bottle of champagne and stood it on his desk.

"This was over from Christmas. You take it home. Open it as soon as you get inside the door. Say you heard from me Anna wasn't well, and you bought it as a tonic. You don't need me to tell you what to do then. Let her talk, and don't say much; let her cry, it'll do her good. She may say things she shouldn't, but underneath it'll please her you thought of the champagne. And don't forget, dear, you're too young and too clever to get in a rut. Maybe a glass of champagne will help you to think of a way out. I don't often have a glass of anything, as you know, but when I do it surprises me how clever I seem. Good night, dear. God bless you."

When Emma reached home she found Dad cooking the supper. This had happened so seldom, and only when some major event had upset their lives, that she was quite overcome. Without waiting to take off her outdoor things, she ran to him and took the saucepan and wooden spoon out of his hands.

"Whatever next! Couldn't you have sat down quietly with your paper? You knew I wouldn't be long." Dad raised an eyebrow.

"Did I? I came home and I found the front room looking as if a bomb had hit it. Well, I said to myself, my old girl must have been interrupted, for she'd never leave a room like that. Then I go into the dining-room. What do I see? The little cupboard isn't shut properly. I look in and I find the Christmas champagne gone. Well, I said to myself, if my old girl's drunk all that she won't feel so good when she comes in; I better get on with the supper." Emma hated interference in her kitchen. She didn't like Dad cooking his own supper; it wasn't right after his day's work. She threw aggravated glances round for spots on her stove and general mess, but there was none. But that only made her feel more cross; properly tiring, upsetting day it had been, and to find Dad messing about with the supper capped everything. She said fiercely:

"Sharp, aren't you? Proper old Sherlock Holmes. Can't leave a room half done or take a bottle from a cupboard but you come nosing it out."

Dad's eyes twinkled, but he did not want to upset Emma further, so he kept amusement out of his voice. "What's the news? I take it the balloon's gone up."

"You take it right. Had Anna here all day. Hysterics and that. She'd seen Ruth and Paul get into a car."

"So'd Charles. From the sound of it, everybody saw her get in but us."

"Doris said seeing that must have sent her crackers; those were her very words. I was surprised at Doris. Very helpful she was and sensible."

Dad looked anxious.

"Not upset? Pity. I had Andrew along to 'The Green Man' to-night especially to let him see how angry I was at the idea of film-actin' for Paul. Don't want Doris makin' nothing of it, or we'll never get those christenin's through. Anna had the champagne?"

Emma glanced at the clock.

"Having it by now. I gave it to George to take to her." She stopped stirring to look at Dad. "Things are bad there. George is a bit low; I went to see him in his office."

"Serve him right; shouldn't have married the silly little cat."

"Too late for that now. What we've got to do is to help them over this bad patch; there's the children to think of. Got to think how to make Anna happier. I was telling George to have a talk with you. He's in a rut, and he knows it. I was sure you'd have an idea what he should be at—outside his work, I mean. Something that would bring Anna into things a bit. Did you speak to Peter?"

Dad had meant to keep that tit-bit until later. He had pictured telling Emma about it when she was not busy and had time for a good laugh; but he could not evade her direct question.

"This is goin' to kill you. Charles had a talk with Peter—" Dad could not get through his story without laughing. He wiped his eyes as he finished. "Did you ever hear the like? I've heard of some funny ways of comin' by a baby, but this beats everythin'."

Throughout the day Emma had felt increasingly that her family's affairs were on the brink of tragedy. It was difficult to see any part of them as funny. But presently her lips curled upward, then she began to shake, finally she had to lean against her stove.

"Dad, you are a one—Peter never could have thought that—well, if that doesn't beat everything . . ."

Dad gave his eyes another wipe.

"Charles says he reckons he ought to patent the idea, there'd be money in it; but if Peter had an idea of how to stop one comin', there'd be millions in it."

Emma dished up the supper.

"You and the doctor and your common talk." She paused for another chuckle. "Still, it is funny. Start one by film acting! Poor dears! I never heard such an idea."

CHAPTER 5
THE MIST LIFTS

THE letter was explicit. Rose of England Films Incorporated wished to engage Paul at a salary of a hundred pounds a week for four weeks, and after that at twenty pounds a day. The four hundred would be paid in one sum free of income tax, to be put on trust for the child until he came of age, or to be used for his education. Ruth would receive a sum to be agreed, for looking after Paul and for their out-of-pocket expenses. Transport would be provided for Ruth and Paul from their home to the studio or wherever else the company should need the child. If these terms met with Peter's and Ruth's approval, Mr. Dragon asked that he might be answered by telephone, as there was some urgency, and he would like to have the contract drawn up immediately.

Ruth and Peter were amazed. Though they had both accepted that Paul would act in a film, neither of them had given thought to the money angle. Both had known money would be paid; but four hundred pounds! Twenty pounds a day! The letter arrived just as Peter was leaving for the shop.

They read it in the passage, but as the magnitude of Paul's earnings came to them they were drawn towards the kitchen, where they could see Paul eating his breakfast. The table was under the window and the sun was on his hair, which made him look even fairer than he was. He was absorbed shovelling cereal into his mouth. Both parents studied him with new eyes. What had they given birth to? What quality had he that made him worth all that money? Paul became conscious he was being looked at; he beamed at his parents over his spoon. Doing this he seemed more ordinary, and therefore more puzzling. Ruth thought he surely did look cute, and Peter that he wasn't a bad-looking kid. But four hundred pounds! Ruth tried to speak normally, but she could hear a tinge of respect creeping into her voice.

"Eat your cereal nicely, Paul dear."

Peter, to say something natural, spoke with undue firmness.

"His hair's too long."

Ruth was spared explaining that Noel Water wanted it even longer, by Paul.

"Why is you still here, Dad? Aren't you goin' to the shop?"

Peter glanced at his watch; he was a minute or two later starting than usual, but it was no wonder, after receiving a letter like that. He went into the kitchen, kissed the top of Paul's head, then signalled to Ruth to come with him to the front door. Up to the arrival of the letter, having looked at Paul's film-acting simply as a means to an end, he had been satisfied to leave arrangements to Ruth; but with all this money attached things were different.

"I'll have to telephone about this, of course. I mean it better be me, with all this money about."

Ruth, after a twitch of surprise, for she had come to look upon everything to do with *Cast a Stone* as her business, was pleased. It was nice to have Peter shouldering the money side.

"Why yes, dear, I think you should."

Peter, though he would not have admitted it for the world, felt shy at the thought of ringing up a film studio. He tried to cover his shyness by an off-hand tone.

"Who shall I speak to? This fellow Dragon?"

His tone did not deceive Ruth for a moment. She knew his saying "This fellow Dragon" was just a little boy bragging. She took the fountain-pen out of his pocket.

"I expect when Mr. Dragon hears it's you he will want to speak to you himself, but I should ask for his secretary." She took the letter from him. "Her name is Miss Mona Bun. I'll write it across this corner. She's just darling, and she will be so pleased you called up." She gave him the letter and put the pen back in his pocket, then, linking her arm through his, she walked with him to the gate.

"What are you going to do about your father? I'm afraid he's not going to be pleased."

Peter made a face.

"Too true, he won't. I shall show him the letter. No good beating about the bush. Anyway, who cares what he or anyone else thinks?" He kissed her and squeezed her arm. "We know it's important."

Ruth returned his kiss and his squeeze, but she went back into the house puzzled. It was just wonderful Peter was so happy about this film, but it was unnatural. She wished she knew why. Could he have read *The Mind and the Child* and just be pretending that he had not?

Dad-Tring had a deep respect for inherited or earned money, and a deep distrust of money easily come by.

Being English, he could not resist having a bit on a horse for the classic races, but the only pleasure he got out of a win was the admiration of his cronies in his sharpness at picking the winner; the sum won he got rid of at once, usually standing drinks at "The Green Man", for he was glad to see the back of it. He was alone in the room behind the shop when Peter arrived and, feeling he might as well get it over, gave him Mr. Dragon's letter. As he put on his glasses and saw the film company's name on the top of the paper, he prepared himself to give his rehearsed speech on film-acting, but as he read the letter real anger and disgust swept over him.

"Are they daft? Payin' four hundred pounds to a kid. Half a crown a week would have been too much. No wonder we always hear films are losin' money; stands to reason no business can waste money like that. Four hundred pounds! Twenty pounds a day! You tell em what they can do with their four hundred pounds."

"Ruth and I have decided to accept the offer."

"Accept! Are you mad, both of you? I tell you no good will come of money made like that."

Peter made a move to say that it was not the money, but Dad was not to be interrupted; he had to make his planned speech and, though the need to pretend to be upset was over, he must say some of the things he had intended. That it was disgusting; a grandson of his a film actor. Making a sissy of the boy; have him ballet-dancing next; but, because it had really shocked him, he kept returning to the money theme. Money was a serious matter; it was terrible to think of it being strewn around like confetti.

"Four hundred pounds! Twenty pounds a day! Who do they think they're paying? The Archbishop of Canterbury?"

Peter let the storm blow itself out. He hated quarrelling with his father, for he liked peace, and they had to work together, moreover, he was fond of him and disliked upsetting him; but he was supported by his secret knowledge of why he was accepting the film company's offer. He would dearly have liked to have told Dad his reasons; he wouldn't agree probably, but he would at least have seen it was not money or fame which had tempted him. However, the doctor had said he was not to discuss his motive with anyone, so he wouldn't; he had not even talked of it openly with Ruth, though it was clear she had somehow cottoned on to the same idea; hadn't she said "I knew this was important?" "Shout as much as you like, Dad," he thought, "you won't change my decision. A change is just what Ruth needs to start a baby, and it was your friend Charles who told me so."

Andrew, as he parked his bicycle at the back of the shop, heard Dad's raised voice. "I'll keep out of that," he thought. He tried to creep in without making any noise, but Dad heard him and, following the plan to involve his whole family, yelled to him to come in. He tossed Peter's letter to him.

"Ever read such nonsense? Four hundred pounds! Disgustin'. No wonder the country's rottin' away. No respect for money. Twenty pounds a day for film-actin'!"

Andrew read the letter as slowly as he could, wondering what to say. Evidently, from the row, Peter was going to let Paul do the film-acting. Doris was a clever one; she had said he would, and that without knowing anything about the money offered. She had said too there would be this row and he was to be neutral. Maybe Doris, if she were here, would see a way to be that; but he was blessed if he knew how. One word in favour of Peter and he would be accused of being on Peter's side. He spoke hesitantly:

"I know how you feel, Dad, and I agree, of course; but four hundred pounds free of income tax is not to be sneezed at. I shouldn't like Jimmie in a film, but with all that for him I should have to think a lot before I said 'No'—you see, it can be spent on his education . . ."

Dad, looking like the cliffs of Dover in a thunderstorm, let out a hiss like an explosive soda-water syphon. There was nothing feigned about his temper. Everything had gone wrong. Peter was letting Paul act in a film which he never would have done if he hadn't persuaded Charles to speak to him, and what good was coming out of it? None. Andrew should be angry. Hadn't the whole idea been to stir up a family row, so that he could get Doris and Anna coming to him for sympathy, which would mean Doris getting so fond of him that to please him she would have the boys christened? And here was Andrew, the mealy-mouthed idiot, taking Peter's side. That, on top of the disgusting money business, was too much.

"You're a fool, Andrew. You always were. You would take Peter's side. You haven't the guts to be angry. You would see good in money earned that way. Could be used for education! So could stolen money. So could money earned by forgin' a cheque; but does that make good money? The film business is rotten all through, and you know it, but you're too mealy-mouthed to say so. If the whole business wasn't rotten would they pay a baby four hundred pounds? Just throwin' money away; want to get rid of it, I suppose."

Andrew tried another move towards neutrality.

"I didn't say I liked the film business . . . I only meant—" Lost for words, and afraid of making matters worse, he took his white coat off its hook, and started to put it on.

"Oh—well . . . I better go and open up."

Dad let out another syphon noise.

"You'll do nothin' of the sort. Mr. Peter Tring can do that, if he's not too grand, seein' I can't afford to pay him twenty pounds a day."

Andrew forgot to be neutral.

"I say, Dad, that's . . ."

Dad banged on the table.

"You shut up! This business is between Peter and me. If you can't keep quiet, go home." As he said the words Dad grasped their wisdom. "Yes, go home—you go to that wife of yours—you tell her what the letter said—she's full of talk of equality and that—you see what she says about payin' a kid of four a hundred pounds a week. Go on. As for Peter, no matter what his boy earns he's still employed by me, and he'll do what I tell him, and that's to open up the shop or anythin' else I choose. Off you go now, and don't forget, tell Doris what I've said, and let me know what she says. I think you'll find she'll agree with me."

Left alone, Dad changed into his white coat and combed his hair. Presently his anger began to simmer down; he was still upset about the money, but he fancied he had inadvertently been pretty sharp. He gave his reflection in the wall mirror a satisfied nod. He wasn't doing so badly, after all. It was smart to think of sending Andrew off to his Doris. She was a one for what she called distribution of wealth. She'd have a piece to say about paying four hundred pounds to Paul, and she wouldn't be able to run fast enough to tell the news to Anna. If Mrs. "Jist-Fency" was upset before, what would she say when she heard about four hundred pounds free of income tax? With a little care and tact he'd have both girls eating out of his hands before the week was over. He gave his reflection another nod and spoke to it. "A funny way to the christenin's, old fellow, but if it comes off it's worth it."

Doris's intention to stay neutral had a shaking when she heard Andrew's news. She knew, in spite of all the reactionaries of the Dad-Tring type could do to prop it up, the age of privilege was sinking to its close. She knew that in the new age, of which she would scarcely live to see the conception, much less the birth, the service a man or woman could give to the world would place how they were valued by the world. There would be no more inherited positions; every child would start at scratch, and laurels would be worn by those most fitted to wear laurels. Handing out large rewards for nothing at all must disappear entirely; there was far too much of it, and to her it smelt of Communism. Information was constantly seeping through from Russia of a world of privilege of which England at her worst had scarcely dreamt—a world in which artists and planners got everything and the workers, without whom there would be no Russia, got comparatively nothing. Doris, who in her university days had dabbled in Communism, blushed to think she could have had even a short period of such half-baked thinking. Hearing of the money to be earned by a baby like Paul therefore made her every bit as mad as it made Dad, and she was just as shocked.

"Four hundred pounds! It's disgusting. It makes you ashamed to think there are still such fools in the world—"

"That's almost exactly what Dad said. That's why he told me to tell you; he said you'd agree with him."

That made Doris think. Agreeing with Dad-Tring! Since when? She had seen Andrew arrive home through the kitchen window, and was talking to him leaning on the sill. Now, as he spoke, she looked at him, seeing him from a new angle. He was leaning on his bicycle; behind him she could see Jimmie leaning in much the same position on his toy motor-car; there seemed at that moment very little difference in their ages. Jimmie had stopped pedalling his car round the garden to gaze at Andrew; what did his Dad coming home mean? Andrew was gazing at her; what did his being sent home when he should be at work mean? She smiled, and as she smiled she saw the ludicrousness of the fuss about Paul and his earnings. It was wrong in a world aiming at fair shares for all that any industry should hand out large sums in such an inconsequent way, but she could not prevent it, and so it was not worth being upset over. Poor Andrew! it was nothing to do with him, but he looked as though he was expecting a scolding.

Andrew was encouraged by her smile.

"I did try and remain neutral like you said, but the old man was in such a taking . . ."

"There's nothing to worry about. You go back now and tell your father he's quite right; I agree with him it's the most awful nonsense paying all that money to Paul."

"What shall I say to Peter?"

Doris shrugged her shoulders.

"Say what you like." She whistled. "Four hundred pounds! Wait until Anna hears."

"And money for Ruth, and a car . . ."

Doris fought a stab of jealousy not altogether successfully.

"Don't rub it in. I don't want to take sides . . . in fact I won't take sides; but I must say it's galling to think of Ruth . . ."

"I wouldn't be old George when Anna hears."

"I'll ring your mother. She better tell her. And don't forget to tell Dad-Tring he was quite right. It's about the first time we have agreed about anything, so he may as well hear about it."

Before Doris could ring her, Emma was at her door.

"Oh, Doris dear, I'm just on my way to Anna. Ruth's rung me, Paul's . . ."

Doris stopped her.

"Don't tell me. I've heard from Andrew. Dad-Tring was having a row with Peter about it, and Andrew, trying to take the middle way, put his foot in it and was sent home in disgrace to tell me what he'd done."

"What do you think?"

"Morally or for myself?"

Emma looked blank so Doris went on: "Morally it's disgraceful—in fact I hear for once I'm entirely in agreement with Dad-Tring. Four hundred pounds to a child of four. And for what? For myself I was trying, as you arrived, to get a grip on myself. My lower and baser nature is mad with jealousy; I could bite the kitchen stove when I think of Ruth lording it in a car with a chauffeur, while I foot-slog pram pushing."

Emma looked white and anxious.

"You're a great comfort, dear. I knew you'd be sensible; that's why as soon as I heard I ran to you for advice. Do you know anything about compensation?"

"Compensation for what?"

Emma tried to recall the phrases.

"I'm not sure I'm putting it right; but if a child, or I think a grown person, needs something, it's as if Dad and myself were always quarrelling living in one house."

"Why would you and Dad quarrel?"

"We wouldn't, dear; that's just to explain . . . it's like being hungry . . ."

"What is?"

"Needing approval and admiration . . . and what you need for it is compensation . . . sometimes with a girl a new frock, or a string of beads will do, but I don't think they'd do for Anna; I wish they would, for I saw such a pretty string made like flowers at Littleton's."

The words "approval" and "admiration" struck a spark in Doris's memory . . . in her university days someone had used those words . . . Who was it and what was the connection? Suddenly it came to her: a rather waffley boy, she had forgotten his name but she remembered he had wanted to be a psycho-analyst but failed.

"Have you been seeing a trick cyclist?"

The words startled Emma from her mental fumblings.

"A what, dear?"

"It's the usual phrase for a psycho-analyst."

"Of course not. Just imagine me!" Emma flushed nervously; she must not, in her anxiety for Anna, betray Ruth's secret... "It's just things somebody said ... It was about a child and his school ... But I thought it's what Anna needs ... I mean that compensation ..."

"You mean you want to find something to compensate Anna for Ruth's child being used in a film, instead of hers?"

Emma was grateful.

"How clever you are, Doris! You understand at once and put things so well... That's what I was trying to say. I wondered if a new hat, or George taking her to stay somewhere like those advertisements of France ..."

"Monte Carlo?" Doris wandered to the window and looked out unseeingly, her whole mind focused on the problem. Presently she swung round to Emma. "Nothing like that would be any good. It would only be a palliative. What Anna needs is something happening here that would boost her self-esteem, make her feel a person of importance."

Emma gave a little squeal.

"Oh! Dear Doris, I knew you'd help ... I was so worried ... George ... well, I think I know what to do ... It's something somebody said ... It would be splendid and for George too ... Good-bye, dear ... I must run ... I don't want Anna to hear about the contract from a stranger."

Doris went thoughtfully about her housework. She was not interested in Emma's scheme for compensating Anna—nothing, she thought, could compensate Anna—but she was interested in the bits of psychoanalysis Emma had picked up. Where had the old thing heard them? It was all out of the picture ... Then an idea flashed to her. Of course! Blind fool that she was . . . that would be the answer. She ran to the kitchen and hung out of the window and called Jimmie.

"Paul's going to act in a film. He's going to earn a lot of money. Won't they be surprised at school when they hear?"

Jimmie took it for granted his mother was surprised and shocked. Had she not said that Paul was spoilt and needed toughening?

"Paul will be very silly in a film, won't he, Mum? . . . I expect he'll cry, don't you, Mum?"

It was against Doris's conscience to act dishonestly with children, but she had to and Jimmie would not suffer for he would never know.

"How will he cry? You show me."

Jimmie was delighted to make a noise. He gave a fairly accurate though exaggerated imitation of Paul, as he had seen him kicking and screaming on the floor of the school cloakroom. Doris bore the display for a few seconds only.

"That's enough. Now show me what you and the other boys would do if he cried at school."

Jimmie strutted round shouting:

"Pauly Pauly perambulator! Feeble, feeble . . . ! Silly show-off Pauly. . . Paul's a fish."

For a long time after Jimmie was back playing with his toy motor-car Doris stood at her kitchen window. Outwardly she looked as usual. Inwardly something strange was happening. She, who had always known the answers, was facing the knowledge that she could be hopelessly wrong. That perhaps she could not always slice people up with complete certainty; that it might be that certain slices, even perhaps all the slices, fell into the wrong boxes. Mentally she picked the slices of Ruth out of the boxes in which she had always kept them, and considered new boxes. But what? Presently she went back to her housework with the strangest words in her mind. She, who had always known the answers, found her subconscious saying remarkably clearly, "I don't know where Ruth belongs, because I don't understand her." Emma, between leaving Doris and arriving at Anna's house, planned exactly what she would say, with the result that she arrived looking outwardly composed. She needed composure. There were many who would have liked to have told Anna the news. It had taken no time to spread; Ruth, no longer tied to silence, had told a neighbour, and that neighbour had told a neighbour; the girl cashiers at Tring's gave slightly inaccurate accounts to each customer as they paid their bill. Dad, Andrew and Peter, when asked, had verified the story, Dad embellishing it with his talk on wasted money and what the country was coming to. The neighbour who had actually told the news to Anna had a legitimate excuse for calling. "I've got to pop in sometime," she told her cronies; "she promised me the refusal of any of Geoffrey's castoff school things." An envious voice said, "Lucky you. I'd give a lot to see her face." There were giggles. "So would I; we'll have less of Mrs. 'Stuck-up-jist-fency' now, I shouldn't wonder. She was so certain her Wendy was the only child in the place who would be looked at."

Anna's tears were over; she was packing in a blind, hysterical way, throwing things into cases, only to throw them out again. Iris, in a thrilled whisper, described to Emma what was happening.

"You never saw nothin' like it. Creatin'! 'Bring down me suit-cases, Iris,' she says. "'Ow many?' I asks. 'All the damn lot,' she says. 'I'm takin' everythin'; I'm never comin' back.' I been up outside 'er room once or twice and it's smash—bang—crash, like as if the road was bein' took up—and talkin' to 'erself, she is—and that's a bad sign—'Talk to yourself,' my mother says, 'and the next thing you know you're shut up for ever'—and she looked so queer. 'Oh, Mrs. Tring,' I says to 'er, I says, "ave you come over queer?' Then she says all very posh, 'No; why, Iris?' 'Well,' I says, 'you look very rough,' and she does look rough, same as my Aunt Min when the copper told 'er Uncle was killed by a bus . . ."

Emma silenced Iris and knocked on Anna's door.

"Can I come in, dear?"

Anna's voice was shrill.

"What do you want? If you've come to talk me round it's no good. I'm going, and I'm never coming back."

Emma opened the door. She saw that the floor was covered with clothes, but that very little had actually reached the suit-cases.

"Are you going home?"

"Yes."

"Taking the children?"

"Of course. You didn't think I'd leave them to be kicked around in this hole, did you?"

"What about George?"

Anna's voice rose again.

"He's had his chance. He can't expect me to spend my life in this one-horse place without a soul of my sort in it." Emma knelt on the floor beside Anna. She picked up garments and folded them, and laid them one on top of the other. They were ready if Anna wished to put them either in a suit-case or in a drawer. She kept her voice low and on a soothing note, and though Anna at first interrupted frequently, she went quietly on. She told of her visit to George, and laughed at his plan of a Devon visit. She spoke as if Anna's departure was a certainty, and in her position of departing wife she could confide in her. She told her some of the things George had said, including how fed up he was, and gave to him the credit for the idea that he needed more outside interests.

"Oh dear, I did want to tell him something, but I couldn't; it's Dad to tell him when the time comes. But you know how it is with your Geoffrey; you can't bear to see him looking down in the mouth, can you? Well, that's how I felt about George. I wanted to give him a kiss and say, 'Don't look like that, Georgie. You wait, there's something wonderful coming yours and Anna's way that will soon cure that fed-up feeling . . .'"

Anna was at last attending.

"What's coming?"

"Well, of course I can't say, dear, George must wait for Dad to do that—I'd like to give you a hint, but Dad would never forgive me—besides, it doesn't concern you really, as you're going . . ." She put her hands to her mouth. "Oh!"

"What is it?"

"Your going! I wonder if that will make any difference?"

"Why should it?"

"Well, I don't know. I think it might. The wife's very important in it too."

Anna had some colour back in her cheeks.

"Important?"

"Yes." Emma sat back on her haunches, smiling. "That's what I came to tell you; I hoped to get here before you heard about Paul's film contract. I can't tell you what it is—you must wait for Dad for that—but I can promise you this: if what I believe is coming to you turns up, you wouldn't look at a few weeks' film contract for Wendy; this is something really important, and it's not just for five weeks, it may be for years."

"You aren't saying this to try to stop me leaving?"

"Partly I am, of course. I knew this news about Paul would upset you; I thought you might even think of running away, and so, before you did anything you'd be sorry for, I wanted to drop a hint." Anna gazed at Emma. She might look down on her mother-in-law, but she found she could not distrust her. Then the unkind voice of the woman who had called to tell her the news rang in her ears. She shuddered and buried her face in her hands.

"I can't go on. Everyone's laughing at me."

"If you go on as usual, and let them all see you don't care, it will be a great help to you if what I believe is coming turns up."

Anna raised her head.

"You swear that?"

Emma shook her head.

"I never swear, dear, and I don't intend to start now. Come on, Anna, let's put these things away, and then I've got a little plan. How about me having the children for the day and you slipping up to London to see your mother, and, while you're there, how about a new hat? I've heard it said a new hat is a wonderful help when you're out of spirits. I never tried it myself—I never really like a hat until it's old—but I've had a wonderful lot of comfort from a new saucepan."

It was touch and go. Emma saw the thoughts pass across the girl's face like the shadows cast by clouds on downland.

"You do really promise this . . . well, this something important is going to change things for us?"

"I promise I believe it's on the way; I can't be more positive than that."

"I can't get a hat; there are such a lot of things the children need."

Emma opened her bag.

"I thought of that. Dad always has a bit tucked away for an emergency. Here's five pounds; you have a good time, and buy something pretty."

"Five pounds! I couldn't take five pounds. What will Dad say?"

"He'll be pleased, dear. Spend most of it on the hat. You're going to need smart hats soon." Anna looked almost happy.

"Smart hats! Oh, I do wish you wouldn't be so mysterious. Tell me. I won't tell George."

Emma began to collect the clothes and put them back in their drawers and in the cupboard.

"You won't get any more out of me. You try seeing what you can get out of Dad, and when you come to see him, wear the new hat and give him a kiss for it. He'll like that: he's still an old fool about a pretty face."

Ruth lay relaxed in the crook of Peter's arm, her cheek against his shoulder.

"You're not worrying, dear, are you? Of course it's most unfortunate you have had to quarrel with Dad-Tring; but I guess if he's unreasonable it just had to be."

Peter roused himself from dreamy contentment.

"I wasn't worrying. Dad'll get over it." He laughed. "Being out with us has caused a family get-together. Doris came to the shop to-day, none of your high-hat stuff, but laughing away over the counter."

"Did Anna come?"

"No, but Mum did with Anna's kids. Anna's gone to town for the day . . . Mum said Anna and George would be coming to supper on Sunday. Doris was still in the shop, and she asked her and Andrew. Nobody even looked at me."

Ruth snuggled closer to him. She did not need anyone else, but it was nice to feel close to him when he seemed all you had.

"Mum-Tring has been very sweet and kind, but she does not care for film business, and now everything's settled I fancy she reckons to side with Dad; but it isn't like her someway to pick on anyone—I mean even to please Dad-Tring."

"Can't blame her. You'd side with me, wouldn't you?"

"I would too. Still, I can't help feeling a bit lonesome." Peter kissed her.

"You won't have time to feel lonely popping off to the studio. Mum was all right when you told her, wasn't she?"

"Why yes—she's always just darling; but I could tell she wasn't thinking of me right then. It was as if . . ." Ruth broke off, hunting for words which would make Peter hear the remoteness that had come into his mother's voice. "Well, as if she had said good-bye before a journey, maybe, and we were gone and she was fixing her life without us."

Peter drew her to him.

"What do we care? We know what we want, don't we?"

Doris lay beside Andrew, her face turned to the window, through which she could see the moon.

"Your father is a comic. You know he thinks because I told him the four hundred pounds was nonsense that we share our reasons for thinking it nonsense."

Andrew was happier than he had been for a long time.

"I liked seeing you and the old boy laughing together in the shop. I was glad you said we'd go to supper on Sunday. It was nice of you; it'll please him."

Doris rolled her head to face him.

"I'm not going because of your father, but because of your mother. I don't like leaving the children with a baby-sitter, and you know it; but I will this once, for she interests me. I think she's pretty deep, you know, and it's given me a jolt. I hate being wrong about people."

Andrew did not like disagreeing with Doris, but he spoke without time for thought.

"Mum isn't deep."

"Isn't she? Then what has she said to make Anna go off to London looking reasonably pleased? I met Iris taking the children round to your mother's, and she told me, and she also told me that until your mother turned up Anna was creatin' . . . that's Iris's expression, which meant, I gathered, she was saying she was leaving for good, packing, and talking to herself."

"That wouldn't mean anything; all women say they'll pack and go at some time, don't they?"

"I never have, and when I do you take it from me I'll mean it, and go. There are other things which interest me—psycho-analysis, for one thing . . ."

"What! Mum?"

Doris did not answer that.

"And what on earth could she be doing in 'The Green Man'?"

Andrew could not believe that.

"Mum! Never. She says she's tight if she has a sip of champagne at Christmas."

"I didn't say she was having a drink, I said she was there. Actually she was sitting in the garden at the back; I saw her from a window in Littleton's."

"What, all alone?"

"No, with George and Anna's children and the doctor."

"The doctor!"

"Don't worry; she wasn't talking to him about health. That's one of the reasons I say she's deep, because I'd swear from the look of them they were scheming."

"About what?"

"That's what I hope to find out when we go to supper on Sunday."

George was asleep. Anna could just see the outline of his face in the moonlight. It was a clever face, and handsome; that was one of the reasons she had fallen for him, and he had certainly looked wonderful in uniform. Not that he didn't look all right in civvies, but he could look better. If Mum-Tring was right—and it was impossible to believe she would make a story up—he would have to go to a good tailor; he ought to have clothes that made him look like Anthony Eden. She would have to have good clothes too. She was glad she had bought that *Vogue*, it was a help to have ideas; no good finding yourself unprepared. It really was a lovely hat. She was glad she had bought it before going home. Mummie had been crazy about it; she had said it was sweetly pretty, and it was too. Anna looked at George. He was deeply asleep; nothing would disturb him. She got out of bed and went to her cupboard and took out the hat. She pulled aside the curtain and peered at the dim outline of her head in her hand-mirror. She could not see herself properly, but she knew she looked lovely; it was such a sweet hat. George had been surprised when she said she would love to go to supper with his parents on Sunday and would get Iris to stay with the children; but, then, George didn't know his Dad had paid for the hat. It would be fun letting Doris see it. It would be fun letting everyone see it. What a snub, expecting her to be upset about Paul, and then meeting her in this hat; that would show them. She would be nice but distant; that would be the thing. If something important was coming to them she would have to be like that all the time; the sort of people they knew would be the first to get pushing if they had half a chance. She bowed to the moon. "Hallo. How are you? I know, it is ages since we met, but you know how it is—in our position . . ."

Dad and Mum lay in their favourite positions, Dad on his back, Mum on her side facing him. They had laid in those positions so often over the years that the mattress had dented to fit them. Dad chuckled.

"I think I'll get some champagne; quite an occasion; she agreed with me and admitted it."

"You're a clever old thing. You'll have those boys christened in no time. I don't know how you'll feel about champagne, dear; I knew you would wish to spend a bit, so I gave Anna five pounds from you for a hat . . ."

"A hat! Five pounds!"

"Yes, dear. I wouldn't have been so generous, but I knew you would; you're such a kind old thing. I think, mind you, it was wise, for it got her to London; but you can't manage champagne too."

Emma could not see it in the darkness, but Dad's chin jutted upwards.

"Who says I can't?" He thought a moment. "Doris ought to have a hat too."

Emma could not see Doris accepting five pounds for a hat.

"So she should, but I know what's in that clever old head; you're thinking you'll wait to give it to her until the christenings."

Dad was getting sleepy.

"That's right . . . ought to have a new hat for a christenin' . . ."

"I'll have a chicken for Sunday . . . I'll do it that way you like cold. With the trifle and that. . ." Emma stopped, interrupted by a low rumbling snore; she raised herself and, as she did every night, softly kissed Dad's forehead. "God bless you, old dear. Sweet dreams." Then she lay back and smiled. "I hope he dreams of the right things; he's got a busy time ahead of him."

CHAPTER 6
"A Fine Night . . . And All's Well"

THE studio world surprised and disturbed Ruth. She realised nobody intended to make her feel unwanted, but its make-up did make her feel just that. Noel Water was head of a kingdom composed of writers, actors, and technicians of all types. In his kingdom his people seemed to have an easygoing understanding and acceptance of one another and to live by laws, easily comprehended even by Paul, but which were not supposed to be understood by those outside. In Noel's kingdom everyone used Christian names, but when they stepped out of it to speak to her it was "Yes, Mrs. Tring", "No, Mrs. Tring". A nice woman called Alice, who would later give lessons to Robert Dram, was engaged to look after Paul. Alice had, on the first day's filming, announced herself to Ruth in the most matter-of-fact way, as if it was natural Ruth should need an outsider to look after her child.

"Good morning, Mrs. Tring. I'm Alice. I shall be keeping an eye on Paul for you between takes. I'm a governess really, but I got bored with it and for fun became a film super; when the Rose of England Company found out I was a governess they engaged me to teach an American child who was filming over here, and I've been governess to film children on and off ever since. When there's no child to teach I'm a super again. Hullo, Paul." She held out a hand. "Come and look at the set."

Ruth tried not to sound an interfering mother, but she felt like one, so it was not easy.

"I guess I better come too. Paul's not used to strangers." Paul hung happily on Alice's hand.

"Can I go in the boat?"

Alice had heard from Noel about the gondola.

"Not to-day. To-day you are going to be in a house—not a real one, of course, a pretence one." She turned to Ruth graciously. "Of course come too. The reason someone like me has to be about is that you wouldn't know where you might take him to play, and when he had to be quiet and all that."

Ruth soon learnt that someone like Alice was necessary. For days she scarcely dared move from wherever she first sat down. Not that everyone was not charming to her, when they had time to notice her, for she was Paul's mother, and, as such, to be considered and respected; but only when they had time, and that was seldom. In the end she learned when she could move and when she must keep quiet, and discovered that nobody minded where she went, for, by some means, that she was the mother of the child in Noel Water's picture had been flashed to every person employed by the Rose of England Corporation, so no one questioned her comings and goings; but equally nobody cared, whereas they cared intensely about everything to do with Paul, and, because they cared, seemed to draw him more and more into their world and farther from hers. Ruth, wandering up and down passages, peering at different sets, eyeing with awe the various goings-on, held long, one-sided conversations with her friend, the author of *The Mind and the Child*. She told him over and over again how Paul was reacting, and queried if that was what he would approve. "There's no question but he is wonderfully happy. If there was a tendency to neurotic infantilism—which was what I feared—that surely is cured now. Maybe it was smart to put him into pictures. Maybe that was just what was needed to free his ego, and it surely has done that, for there's no stealing of mother love; right now it sometimes seems he doesn't need me at all. You said he should be compensated, and it seems he is being; but when you wrote that a child would need compensation if he felt he was being torn too soon from his mother's arms, did you mean that he should not need his mother at all? That's the way things are heading right now." One-sided conversations are frustrating. Ruth found that instead of longing that the author of *The Mind and the Child* lived in England rather than America, so that she could have a cosy talk with him, her sub-conscious was wishing for the talk so that she could tell him just what she thought of his advice. Words would float unbidden into her conscious mind. "You may be right about compensation, and certainly Paul is happy and there are no screaming attacks, but maybe the reason is he's just plain spoilt. There are days when he's so upperty to me I could slap him."

Whatever Ruth might think, Noel Water and his crew were charmed with Paul. Noel, slopping around in unpressed grey flannels and a vivid-coloured open-necked shirt, would sweep his hair off his face and say to whoever was by:

"He's a miracle, that child. Tell him a story and it all shows in his little face. He can't put a foot wrong."

Paul was exquisitely happy. He opened like a flower in the atmosphere of approval and admiration in which he found himself. He was a naturally sharp child, but even had he been slow he could not have failed to know eyes were always watching and admiring him, and, had the need arisen, he would have played-up and shown off; but the need had not arisen. Noel did not explain the part of Jonathan as a little boy to him; he was taught what to say, but he let each scene come as a surprise to the child, so that what he felt reflected in his eyes. There were a few scenes for him with his spoilt, selfish, sex-ridden, self-centred stepmother, and his weak, charming father, who was completely under her thumb; but most of his scenes were with the creatures of his imagination. Paul did not like the scenes with his father and stepmother; he half knew they were nice people really, but when he had to say little charming things, or make simple requests, and was either snubbed or disregarded, his hurt at such treatment showed on his face, and when the scene was over it was hard for the actor and actress playing the adults to win back his trust. Noel, watching this, knew how an audience would feel. They would long to hurt the stepmother and pet and comfort the child. They would be glad when his friend the cuckoo clock, the porcelain mandarin, the oak-tree in the garden and the rest of his inmates did the petting and comforting for them. They would think it good when later the child's imagination carried him farther, filling his life with willing slaves who had only to hear him express a wish to rush to fulfil it. Noel was directing the picture in such a way that what the child imagined he saw and heard, the audience could in part see and hear too. This meant that Paul lived in a magic world; nothing was impossible, and that he should feel this was what Noel wished, it was not only on the set that a fairy-tale atmosphere was built up. The film unit, made up mainly of skilled technicians, were charmed to use their talents. Their director—and they were devoted to Noel—wished for conjuring tricks that a child could believe in, and never a day passed but they thought up new ones. Alice had learned from Paul that he expected a big white bird carrying kittens to fly to what he called Noel's house, and in no time the unit's draughtsmen had planned a mechanical bird, the carpenters had built it, the artist had painted it, the wardrobe had contributed a kitten for it to carry, and Alice had Paul standing at the right spot, far enough away for the trickery to be hidden from him, so that he could see the bird fly by flapping its great white wings. One of the camera staff, who in an interval was showing Paul how the camera worked, learned that the child believed that in such a house as Noel's animals could talk. This knowledge was a source of much amusement to the unit, and a never-ending joy to Paul. One of the electricians was a good amateur ventrilo-quist, and by bribery one or other of the film company's cats was always about the set speaking dialogue invented by the unit. Paul, once he had accepted the fact that the cats in Noel's house could talk, added to the fun by answering. As the days passed it was with difficulty that Noel kept the cat dialogue within bounds of decency. Paul only understood the actual words used, and answered politely what he supposed was meant. The ventriloquist electrician started it. One of the cats sidled up to Paul and, on the spur of the moment, he made her ask with unmistakable meaning:

"Going my way, Paul?"

To which Paul answered:

"I can't go anywhere just now, but presently I can."

Discovering Paul's belief in the fairy tale and nurs-ery-rhyme characters, the wardrobe was kept continually busy, so that the child might at any time run into Dick Whittington, Jack and Jill or stumble on Beauty sleeping. Ruth saw some of the fancies arranged for Paul and, though she thought how kind it was of everybody to play with him, it worried her; there did not seem anything she could do about it, but how was she to straighten Paul out when he left this make-believe world? None of the unit nor Alice considered what they might be doing; Paul seemed well and intensely happy, so it seemed to strike none of them that to teach him, at an impressionable age, not to know the difference between fact and fiction was wrong, and Ruth, from shyness and the feeling that nobody cared what she thought, kept her worries to herself.

At the end of two weeks Mr. Dragon, attended by Mona, visited the studio. He had received daily reports on progress, and especially reports on Paul.

He arrived prepared to show that he was pleased. He carried a large parcel to Paul.

"Here is something for you to play with, Paul, when Noel doesn't want you."

The something was a farm. Everything a farm should have was there: animals, trees, fences, and farm buildings. Paul and Alice put it out in a corner of the studio.

"When it's all finished," Paul said, "I s'pose all the animals will walk about, don't you, Alice?"

Alice saw suddenly there might be difficulties ahead. For the first time since she had taken charge of Paul she looked round for Ruth for advice, but Ruth was talking to Mona. Doubtfully she tackled the problem herself.

"I don't think these will, dear."

"Why won't they?"

Alice, torn between her duty to Noel, who had decreed that Paul was to believe that anything was possible, and her training as a teacher, said firmly:

"Mr. Dragon gave you these, dear—it's Noel's things that talk and all that."

This seemed to satisfy Paul for the moment, for he asked no more questions, but quietly arranged his sheep in a ring, nose to tail.

Ruth was delighted to see Mona. Mona, who had been more enthralled every day as news of Paul's success reached the office, was radiant, and, since Mr. Dragon was talking to Noel, and so did not need her, was able to be not the efficient secretary, but just Mona Bun, happy and proud for Ruth.

"Don't you feel just like somebody in a fairy-tale, dear? The romance! Every time I think of what's happened to Paul, almost in the twinkling of an eye as they say, I can't help singing."

Ruth loved Mona's warmth and the fact that she seemed to be pleased to see her as herself, and not as Paul's mother; but as she saw the film only as a means to an end, and a doubtful means at that, she could not share her enthusiasm.

"I suppose everything is going all right. Mr. Water does not talk to me much, but I gather he thinks Paul is making out all right."

"All right! It's much more than all right; they say little Paul's a real find; he should be a sensation. I shouldn't tell you this; but, if Mr. Dram doesn't mind, I believe they are going to give Paul special featuring. Of course little Robert

Dram would have to have it too, but I believe the idea is to say 'Introducing Paul Tring'. Won't you be proud?"

Ruth hated to squash such enthusiasm, but she did not see much to enthuse about. Paul would not read film advertisements, and anyway he surely should have had enough compensation by the time the picture was made. She hoped that by the time it was shown he would just be her own little boy again—only, of course, a different, properly adjusted little boy. It would be best if by that time the means that had been used for the adjusting were forgotten. She was sure the author of *The Mind and the Child* would agree with that.

"I don't know much about movies; I don't think his father and I would want him advertised."

Mona laughed. "Aren't you sweet! Lots of mothers would have got so conceited by now they'd be demanding this and demanding that, but you haven't changed at all." Ruth had to smile at that.

"I just can't imagine any reason why I should have. You've never had a child acting in a movie, so you don't know how low it makes you feel. I'm ignorant of studio ways, of course, and, do you know, little Paul often corrects me. You can't imagine how that makes a mother feel. Why, only last night when I was talking to him I chanced to say how kind the man is who twists the front of the cameras. Paul looked quite shocked and said, as if he were a grown man, 'He's called the focus operator.' He did too. Such words for a little boy to use."

"That just shows how sharp he is. Noel Water says he's too clever to be true. You've seen the rushes, I suppose?"

"No. Mr. Water thinks Paul shouldn't see himself. He doesn't really know about movies."

"But you should see them. You needn't bother; Paul will be quite all right with Alice. You come to the projection-room. This afternoon they're going to run all the takes through, including yesterday's for Mr. Dragon."

Ruth longed to see the rushes, but she disliked this deciding for her what was to happen to Paul.

"I like being about. I never know when I'll be wanted. This picture with talking cuckoo-clocks and trees gives Paul funny ideas. He thinks everything will talk and move if he wants it to."

"But that's splendid; that's just what little Jonathan thought in the book."

"And look what happened to him," said Ruth dryly. "I try to make Paul see it's just a game—I mean things aren't really like that."

"Oh, you shouldn't do that. Mr. Dragon would be most upset if he knew."

"I can't help that. After all, he's my child; I have to think of his character."

"But just being fanciful can't hurt him. I had a funny childhood; I was one of six, and we were brought up very religious—my mother was a preacher. All the others took to religion, but not me. I had a doll and—would you believe it?—I believed she could talk. I used to confide everything to that doll, especially how much I hated hearing Mum preach. But it hasn't hurt me. I haven't gone on thinking dolls can talk."

Ruth hesitated.

"I think it's partly the story worries me. Somehow Paul seems to take to it all so."

"But he isn't like little Jonathan. He had that awful stepmother."

"I know. I expect I'm silly. I think in some ways it's done Paul good being here, only . . ." Ruth broke off, unable to explain her feeling that her son was no longer all hers, and how queer it felt not to be the one to decide what was best for him. "I'm afraid, too, of his getting spoilt. Everybody makes such a fuss of him. That's good in a way, but there can be too much of it."

"He won't get spoilt. Noel Water can be very stern if he wants to. Films cost money. He'd never stand for any naughtiness that wasted time."

"But he wouldn't mind if it didn't waste time."

Mona patted Ruth's knee.

"If you don't mind my saying so, you worry too much."

Ruth managed to smile.

"I expect I do. Anyway, Paul's part will soon be finished."

Mona started to speak, then she changed her mind. She got up.

"Let's have a cup of coffee. And you'll see the rushes this afternoon if I have to drag you there."

Emma was feeling as nearly pleased with herself as she was capable of feeling. She accepted she was not clever, but on this occasion she did think she had handled things pretty well, and—which to her was what mattered—Dad was happy. How he had chuckled in bed after the family Sunday supper.

"I could hardly keep from laughin', Emma. Mrs. 'Jist-Fency' makin' a fuss of me, and all over a hat."

She had answered:

"I suppose it was all about the hat. But it seemed to me more than that, but you'd be the one to know."

Dad had chuckled again.

"Proper makin'-up to me she was. Mind you, Emma, when she comes off her high horse she's a winning little thing."

"She's proud of George in her way; maybe she's got round to it at last that there would be no George if he hadn't a father."

"Or a mother, old dear; you did your share."

She had been silent for a little after that before planting her next idea.

"How did you think George looked?"

Dad never thought how anybody looked.

"Much as usual, wasn't he?"

"Your eyes are sharper than mine. I've thought lately he's a bit depressed. Of course, you'd know more about it than I would, but I was wondering if you couldn't put him on to something which would take him out of himself a bit."

"What sort of somethin'?"

"I wouldn't know, dear; but he needs to meet more people of his own sort, and use that brain of his more. Next time you're in 'The Green Man' you could have a talk with the doctor and see if there isn't something he could be doing. Of course, you know more what's going than the doctor does, but two heads are better than one. I don't think there's enough interesting work coming his way to keep his mind occupied."

Dad had given another low, rumbling chuckle.

"When I was his age I didn't need my mind occupied, you and I. . ."

She had never cared for that sort of talk.

"Now then; now then."

"All right, old dear; but it's true, and you know it. Our Doris is a funny one."

"Deep. But I'm getting fond of her. I seem to like her more each time I see her. She's been wonderfully kind helping over Anna and that. I like to see her eyes twinkle."

"So do I, but I'd like to know what they're twinklin' about, and I'd like to see them twinklin' at a christenin'."

"You and she seemed to be getting on together all right."

"We were, but I don't get down to her somehow."

"You old fraud, you! How much more do you want? There you sat in your armchair with Anna on one arm and Doris on the other; proper old Turk you looked."

Dad had started to laugh, but it was swallowed in a yawn.

"Deep, though. All the time we were jokin' her eyes were dartin' round to see how everybody was gettin' on. And mostly she was watchin' you."

Emma had given him an affectionate pat.

"Get any sharper and you'll cut yourself. If you see the doctor at 'The Green Man' to-morrow don't forget to have a word with him about George."

"'Green Man.' All right . . ."

The sentence had died in a deep, cosy snore. Emma had raised herself on her elbow and kissed his forehead.

"God bless you, old dear. Sweet dreams."

As the days passed Doris's curiosity grew. She was sticking to her resolution not to be drawn into a family squabble, but that did not prevent her being interested in family reactions, and though she did not realise it, this was a change, for she was interested humbly, without supposing she knew the answers. She could not get Emma out of her mind, Emma turned her world upside down. Emma made her question if the way of living and thinking in which she believed so utterly was the only way. Old Emma, with her husband and three sons, looking and behaving like any elderly housewife, was quite clearly, when nobody was looking, pulling all the strings. What was she planning for Anna? What hand had she had in seeing Paul's film contract was accepted? How could Ruth or anybody else have made old Emma think that a psychological necessity? Why, the old thing would not know the meaning of psychology. Yet compensation! Old Emma had got that expression, and some idea of what it meant from somewhere. Sometimes, as she tidied her hygienic house, washed and dressed her hygienic baby, and talked to her brilliant, hygienic Jimmie, a stab of doubt would run through Doris. For all her brains, modern outlook and intelligent thinking, was she as successful a wife and mother as her retrogressive, almost uneducated, mother-in-law?

Andrew, without being conscious of it, increased Doris's inward doubtings. It was a week after the Sunday at his parents when he said:

"Old Dad properly enjoyed himself last Sunday, didn't he? I like to hear him laugh like that."

"I never found out what your mother was doing with the doctor in 'The Green Man'."

"Why didn't you ask her? It would have been no end of a joke."

"She'd have turned it to a joke all right, but she wouldn't have told me the answer, and I don't think she would have liked me asking."

"Mum! Why?"

"Reasons. I tell you she's deep."

Andrew laughed.

"Mum couldn't be deep if she tried."

"Has she changed much as she's grown older?"

Andrew thought this over.

"No. Always been the same." His voice warmed. "Right back as far as I can remember she was cooking or sewing and just lived for us to come home. Same as she does now. But deep. No. You've got her wrong there. Nor would I want her deep, bless her."

Doris gave a lot of thought to Emma and her unseen string-pulling. Would Jimmie and John when they grew up speak of her with the warmth with which Andrew spoke of his mother? Did Andrew enjoy coming home to her as much as his father had always enjoyed coming home to Emma? Could it be there was something to be said for the sort of hominess Emma created, as opposed to a well-sharpened brain in a healthy, well-planned home, which was her contribution to her family's well-being? It was disturbing to be churned up and made to wonder: was she imagining things? In search of proof, she went to visit Ruth.

Since the start of the filming of *Cast a Stone* none of the family had seen Ruth nor heard much about her. Peter never spoke of the film in the shop, nor indeed much at home. It was a means to an end, but not, to him, interesting in any other way. Doris, once she had decided to visit Ruth, did what no other member of the family would have dreamt of doing: she rang up the studio. Ruth had not supposed anyone could ring her up at the studio, but it seemed incredibly simple. She was having the coffee to which Mona had invited her when a page told her she was wanted. Rather flustered, she was directed to the telephone to hear Doris's cool voice on the line.

"It seems ages since any of us saw or heard of you. What time do you get home? I'd like to come round and hear all your news."

Because Doris was a Tring, and so represented normality as opposed to the queer, abnormal film world, a sudden longing came over Ruth for Trings. Asking Doris to wait, she hurried back to Mona. Was it possible for a relation to come to the studio?

Mona was glad to see Ruth behaving more normally. It was to be expected the mother of a successful film child would ask for favours rather than wonder whether film-acting was good for him. She decided this was an occasion to use her own discretion; she could put things straight with Noel and Mr. Dragon later.

"I can arrange it. Why not see if she could come to-day? Just the day, with Mr. Dragon here; besides, it would be a treat for her to see the rushes."

Ruth's voice came almost pleadingly over the phone. "Doris, you come here. I suppose you couldn't manage to-day? It seems they're going to see all of the film that's been taken up to now, and they want me to look. I thought I should look forward to seeing Paul on the pictures, but right now I'm kind of scared."

Through Doris's mind ran plans. Someone to look after Jimmie and John. It couldn't be Anna—no good rubbing Anna's nose in Paul's film; it would have to be Emma. Yes, she would manage it. She knew it was silly of her, but she could not help feeling excited; it would be fun for once to see a film being made.

"I'll make it. Where is it? How do I get there?"

Emma agreed at once to take charge of Jimmie and John, but she was surprised at Doris's request, and when she brought the children round she said so.

"Fancy you off to the studio, Doris. I wouldn't have thought it would be you would want to have a look. I know Anna would if she wasn't too proud to ask."

"It's more that I haven't seen Ruth to know how she's getting on."

Emma did not reply to that, but her quick look of surprise showed that she had not before thought of a close friendship between Doris and Ruth. Doris told her half the truth.

"I'm interested. I want to know what effect, if any, Ruth thinks this film-acting has had on Paul."

Emma too wanted to know that. She had not seen Ruth since the filming started. Was she getting for Paul that compensation she thought he needed, all because she had read some silly book? She did hope so, poor little thing, since she was so certain it was the right thing to do. If Ruth found it all a mistake, and little Paul played up just as he had before, she was going to be disappointed, and, though she would not know it, would have caused a lot of trouble for nothing. As far as she could, she had planned for a wider life for George, and a life she would like for Anna, but it was only plans; if it didn't come off it would be difficult to hold Anna. All the girl had at present was a hint of what was coming; if the hint didn't materialise she would be so unsettled it might break things up for good. The family shake-up might turn out well, but it might turn out disastrously; after all, Dad was counting on only one thing, which was to get Doris's children christened, and that was no nearer happening; he'd worry more about those christenings than ever if, having in his mind half got them to the font, they remained unchristened.

"I'd like to know too how Ruth's getting on. Tell her I wanted to know, will you, Doris dear?"

Doris sounded casual.

"What you'd like to know is how he looks on the films, I expect."

"No. No, dear. I'd like to know the same things you'd like to know. You ask her from me how Paul's getting on ... He'd a little bit of a temper now and then ... Ask her if he's got over that."

Jimmie's imitation of Paul screaming surrounded by cruel small boys was vivid in Doris's mind. That Ruth could imagine this spot-lighting of her child as a cure for an inferiority complex, and succeed in persuading Emma to see it that way, was nothing short of astounding; she must discover the answers.

"You leave it to me. I'll find out exactly how he's getting on, and I'll tell you everything when I come to fetch the boys."

Without warning, Paul began to pack the farm back in its box. Alice thought this a mistake. A gift from Mr. Dragon should be very much in evidence all the time Mr. Dragon was in the studio.

The camera man responsible for studio stills shared this view, and had intended to immortalise the gift by photographing Paul playing with it.

"Don't let's pack it up," Alice suggested. "We could have it out ready to play with this afternoon."

Paul put a cow in the box.

"Puttin' it away."

"Leave the farm out," the stills' man called to Alice. "We're just breaking for dinner now, but I'm taking some stills of him playing with it later."

To Alice—unimportant cog in the great Rose of England Corporation—a mere suggestion from any member of Noel's unit was an order. She laid a restraining hand on Paul.

"Isn't that a good idea! Your farm is going to be photographed. You'd like that, wouldn't you?" Paul appeared not to have heard her or to notice her restraining hand. Deliberately and with concentration he went on packing. "Now, Paul, you don't want poor Alice to have all the trouble of unpacking them again, do you?"

Paul frowned at her.

"They isn't goin' to be unpacked. I'm goin' to give them back to Mr. Dragon."

Alice disguised her horror at this suggestion with a bright laugh.

"What would Mr. Dragon do with a farm?" She looked round for Ruth. She was still with Mona Bun, but it was nearly dinner-time; it would not be a confession of failure to take the child over to her a few minutes early. "Is Paul hungry?" Alice cast an experienced eye at the set. Paul's stand-in was standing for Paul before the grandfather clock, while the distance between him and the cameras was measured and marked in chalk. Noel and his three assistant directors were discussing something with Mr. Dragon. The unit, from the continuity girl to the youngest rigger, had replaced their usual on-the-job expressions for the relaxed ones they wore before the lunch break or in the few minutes before work finished for the day. It was obvious Paul would not be needed until the afternoon. "We won't pack any more of the farm now; we'll go to Mummie to get washed for lunch."

Paul flushed.

"I'm puttin' it away."

If it had not been that at that moment Noel, his assistants and Mr. Dragon had turned, because of some point they were discussing, to look at Paul, Alice would have let Paul have his way. It was her business to keep him happy and amused, not to argue with him; but Mr. Dragon's present! Paul should be happily playing with it, not hurriedly packing it back in its box. She picked up a cow Paul had just packed.

"This moo-cow is my favourite. Which do you like, Paul?"

Paul wanted to put the farm out of sight, to cram the lid on it. It was just a toy, and he had now no use for things that were just toys. He wanted toys only if they belonged to Noel's house and could move and talk. Somewhere, pressing up in him like the shoot of a seed pressing through the earth, was knowledge; knowledge which, when it grew, would kill one by one his beliefs and fancies. He did not know what was growing in him; he just knew that something was there, and that it was something which would tell him things he did not want to know. Because he was frightened of being made to look at his static toy farm, and accept that toys were but toys, he snatched at his animals, fences and outhouses and, without caring if he damaged them, crammed them into their box. His face was crimson. In a half belief that he could make even the toy animals understand, he raised his voice.

"Don't like any of them—nasty, silly animals." He kicked the box. "Don't want beas'ly farm."

Alice, distressed, tried to calm him.

"You don't mean that. It's a lovely farm. Still, we'll put it away now; after lunch Alice will stand it all up again."

Alice could not have chosen a more unlucky statement.

That Alice could, at any moment, lay the hated, unmagic, static farm out in Noel's house, where all should be magic, drove Paul to frenzy. He beat at Alice with his fists.

"You shan't touch it—you shan't—you shan't . . . I hate you, Alice—I hate the farm . . . I'll break it up. I will too—I want Noel's thin's."

Overcome by a feeling of hopelessness in the face of the all-powerful grown-up world, as exemplified at that moment by Alice, he flung himself on the floor kicking and screaming.

William Dragon might be a dragon in behaviour as well as in name in Mona's eyes; but in actual fact, provided it did not waste that appallingly expensive commodity "scheduled time", he was pleasant and tolerant to the foibles of others. The break for luncheon was not scheduled time; the artists, and indeed the whole unit, could spend it as they liked; always provided their way of spending did not interfere with the afternoon schedule. He could clearly remember his own troubled childhood. The torrents of tears that poured out of him when the musical side of his brain was affected by his mother's violin-playing. The struggle to understand what his temperamentally thwarted father was trying to explain when he began to teach him to recite. The wildness, fears and need for expression that were his heritage from the mixed blood of his artistic parents. He felt sure he understood Paul; moreover, that he had got to understand him, lest he was not fit to act in the scene scheduled for the afternoon. He strode across to him, picked him up and gave him to Ruth. He sat down between her and Mona, and spoke conversationally.

"I wonder why Paul screamed, don't you, Mrs. Tring?" Paul reacted to the calm tone.

"I didn't want that farm."

Ruth was shamed.

"Why, Paul, that's a very rude way to talk. Mr. Dragon bought that present especially for you."

Mr. Dragon held up a hand to silence her.

"Why didn't you want it?"

Paul's face had been buried in Ruth's shoulder. He lifted enough of it for one eye to focus Mr. Dragon.

"It's only a toy."

"You don't like toys?"

"In Noel's house there aren't no toys—everythin' talks." Noel was standing nearby.

"He thinks the studio's my house."

Paul raised his head to look at Noel.

"It is your house."

Mona tried to help.

"Of course it is, and a very nice house."

Mr. Dragon nodded approval.

"Of course it is. Could you arrange for the farm to behave as expected in your house, Noel?"

Ruth looked up at Noel pleadingly.

"Please—I think he ought . . ."

Mr. Dragon silenced her with a shake of his head. "There is a lot of work for him to get through this afternoon. Can you fix that, Noel? Good. Now listen, Paul, you go and eat your lunch and stop crying. Noel's taking the farm, and when you next see it all the animals will talk." This planned fairyland was not what Paul wanted, but talking had stopped his tears. He leant rather wearily against Ruth. Mr. Dragon got up. "That'll be all right, won't it? Mona, see Mrs. Tring has everything she wants for Paul." He lifted Paul's chin and smiled at him. "I should ask for something extra nice. What about pink ice-cream with strawberries? You don't know it yet, Paul; but I'll tell you a secret. You are going to be a very important little boy. Come along, Noel."

Mona looked after Mr. Dragon with shining eyes. This was real romance.

"Isn't he wonderful?"

Ruth was going to speak her mind, but at that moment an unexpected thing happened. Noel looked back at her over his shoulder and winked. A wink which seemed to say: "Don't worry. We'll get together about this later on." She turned to Mona smiling.

"Why yes, he's just darling."

In spite of herself, Doris found herself overawed by the Rose of England studios, and especially by the effect of the name Tring. She arrived just as an assistant director was calling for silence, and slipped into a chair beside Ruth's. The lights blazed down on Paul, a voice announced the number of the take. Paul's voice came to her ordering the clock to speak more loudly. Presently someone called

"Cut", and she saw a man cross to Paul and kneel to get on a level with his face.

"That's fine, Paul; but do you think you could sound even grander? You see, now you know they will all do what you order them to do, you must be much grander than you were last week, when you weren't sure if they would obey you."

Paul made a proud face.

"I'll look like this, Noel, an' I'll speak as if I was king." Ruth turned to Doris.

"We can talk now until the next take."

"You'll have a bit of a job with Paul after this, won't you?"

The remark had been made spontaneously. Ruth, shattered by the morning scene, spoke more easily to Doris than she had ever done before. She did not explain about *The Mind and the Child*, but of her present anxieties, culminating with the morning's scene.

"I think it's so terrible to raise a child that way. Why, he just thinks everything can talk and move if he wants it to."

"Can't you tell them you don't like it?"

Ruth saw Doris had no conception of the film world. "You don't know what it's like. It seems nothing matters but the picture. If we get behind on schedule it's as if there'd been a death in the house. That Paul is happy and good in his scenes is all that matters to them; they reckon they've bought him. If I said I thought maybe all this make-believe was bad for his character, I think they would think I was plain crazy. They wouldn't say just that, but what they would think would be, 'What does the child's character matter if it's a good movie?'"

"Why did you let him do it? You must have guessed how it would be."

Ruth hesitated. Should she trust Doris? Then her need for a confidante overran her fear of not being understood.

"Did you ever read a book called *The Mind and the Child* . . . ?"

Doris knew little of psychiatry. She accepted there were psychiatrists and that there were people who needed psychiatric treatment, but she would hate to think that she or any of her family needed anything of that sort. She was proud of the conviction that she never closed her mind to anything; psychiatric treatment was gaining in importance, so of course she was interested in it. In actual fact her subconscious mind considered anyone needing the help of a psychiatrist was "bats". But, as Ruth talked, her mind stretched. She dismissed Ruth's belief that the original screaming attacks came from need to attract attention; she knew what she had always known— that Ruth spoilt her child. But when Ruth came to the part of her story about school and how Paul had "gotten more difficult" she was absorbed. She did not believe in mother-fixation or any nonsense of that sort, but she did believe in an ordinary inferiority complex. Putting Ruth's story together with Jimmie's imitation of Paul and his schoolmates, it could easily be that for some reason he suffered from that. It was a pretty drastic way of curing it, but obviously, if a child felt inferior, putting it to play a star part in a film should cure it.

Ruth's voice wobbled at the end of her story.

"It's so disappointing; you see, it's done no good; he screamed and kicked this morning just as if he hadn't been compensated."

Doris laughed.

"Now you're being silly. When the picture's over the grandeur begins. When he goes back to school he'll be Paul, our film star."

Ruth smiled a rather watery smile.

"You are comforting, Doris. I don't know why it is, but I seem to get so nervous these days. Maybe it's tiring sitting all day in this hot studio, and then, of course, there's the home. I fix it as best I can before I come out, but there's a lot of chores waiting when I get home."

"Can't you get an Iris?"

Ruth caught the twinkle in Doris's eye. She laughed. "Isn't that girl just terrible? I can't figure why Anna has her in the house. I haven't got an Iris, but I have help; but you know the way it goes . . . mostly things you must do yourself if you want them done right, but I'm tired when I get home."

Doris looked at Ruth.

"You do look tired. But you're being silly; you let Paul in for this for a reason I don't really agree with, for I don't look on children as problems . . ."

"That's what Mum-Tring said." Ruth's hand flew to her mouth. "That crazy tongue of mine! I never meant you to know I had told her."

"Don't worry, I guessed. She used the word 'compensation' in connection with Anna; I knew she could never have picked on it. Our mother-in-law is a much wiser bird than I knew."

Ruth was surprised.

"Except for my own mother I always thought she was just the sweetest person I knew."

"Sweet, yes—wise is a different thing."

Ruth patted Doris's knee.

"I am glad you came. I was feeling lower than a snake.

You don't know what it's like here. They're the nicest people, but it seems Paul isn't mine any more."

Mona came towards them.

"Time for the rushes, Mrs. Tring." Ruth introduced Doris. Mona beamed. How wonderful to be Paul's aunt! How exciting for Ruth to see rushes for the first time with her sister-in-law there to admire. How thrilling life was! "I am glad you chose to come to-day Mrs. Andrew Tring. I feel sure Paul is going to have a very proud auntie."

It was a curious experience seeing Paul acting in a film. Like most small children, he acted without effort, and Noel had directed him brilliantly; as well, he had a naturally expressive face, his eyes showed all the innocent wonder, unexplained fears, and absorption in the immediate interests, of the tiny child. Though sequences were missing, Paul's share of the picture was fairly straight as far as it had gone, and Ruth found herself forgetting it was just a film, and that Paul was her son, and was carried away. Although she knew her, in real life, as a friendly creature, with children of her own whom she adored, she was filled with loathing for little Jonathan's sex-ridden, spoilt, self-centred stepmother, and she despised his weak father, though in the studio he was a nice creature who, between shots, sang silly songs to Paul. As she watched the sensitive, highly-strung little Jonathan being turned from a normal child into a child living in a dream world, and from snubs and neglect in his real world, peopling that dream world with slaves, tears ran down her face. Poor child! poor little Jonathan! what chance had a child raised that way? He would not be to blame if he grew up a bad man; the way things were shaping he just must grow up queer; no child must think it right to be treated as a god. The last shot showed the beginning of the disease of megalomania in Jonathan. For the first time he confused his two worlds; straight from the slavish, humble worship of a tree he came in sudden contact with a gardener. He gave the gardener a swift, imperious order, which was overheard by his stepmother and his father. That scene was Noel's triumph. He had succeeded, in the second in which Jonathan realised the gardener was not going to obey him, and before he cringed to his stepmother, in getting an expression of such hatred on the child's face that it was frightening. At that moment, the rushes being over, the lights were turned on. Ruth came back to the projection-room and realised it had been on Paul's face that she had seen evil. She clutched at Doris, whispered, "That was Paul," and fainted.

Everybody had been gripped by the rushes. Noel, who had left the set in charge of his second in command, in order to watch William Dragon's reactions, found he had forgotten William Dragon in his interest in the acting. Mona ceased to remember the romance of Paul's success story, and as the lights came up was wiping her eyes, murmuring "Poor little kid!" Only William Dragon was not excited, but, if anything, worried. As the lights came up Noel saw this, but before he could say anything Ruth's faint created a diversion.

The news that Ruth had fainted ran through the studio and caused immense satisfaction. It was considered a tribute to all concerned. Those who had seen the rushes said they did not wonder—the picture was enough to move anybody, let alone the child's mother. Those who had not seen it reported that Mr. Dragon had sprung to his feet and said, "This will shake the world. This is genius," and that Ruth had not been the only one to feel queer; Mona Bun had been able hardly to stand, and the wardrobe mistress had felt sick for an hour afterwards. Up till that moment Noel had kept the viewing of the rushes to a limited circle. With more general viewing news of Noel Water's new picture rushed round the Rose of England Studios, and before the afternoon was over it was being talked of by other units, and by artists working on other pictures, and watchful eyes were looking for Paul, about whom the word "genius" had been used.

Ruth came round quickly; she refused to go to the first-aid room, but lay down in Paul's dressing-room, and sent Doris back to watch the filming.

"I'm fine now. You go and watch; it's new to you; maybe you'll find it fun." Doris had lingered, wondering whether it would help Ruth to talk. Ruth guessed what was in her mind. "I'd rather be alone for a while. Maybe I can explain in the car going home. I've got to get things straight with myself."

William Dragon and Noel walked up and down an unused set. There had been no need for William Dragon to say much about the film; it was good, and Noel knew it was good. It was trouble they talked about. Children and animals in their pictures were anathema to leading actors. William Dragon was a thoroughly worried man.

"He said he would only do this picture if I kept the child scenes down, though he felt better about them when we decided to use his son. I wouldn't put it past him to chuck up the picture if he sees those rushes."

Noel felt what was coming. He dug his nails into his palms—a trick when he needed to keep his temper.

"He needn't see them," William Dragon answered with a raised eyebrow. Noel dug his nails into his flesh until they hurt. It was obvious Nicholas Dram would hear about Paul. Film gossip travels fast. He might say he would throw up the film. If he did there was no doubt what would come next. It would be tactfully done, but the cutting room's scissors would be cut clipping Paul almost to nothing . . . as an artist, that, to Noel, was unthinkable. Those few scenes with Paul were perhaps the finest he had ever directed or would ever direct. He did not need to explain how he felt. William Dragon might be a great film executive, but he was also an artist. "I couldn't scrap them."

"How many more scenes are there for the child?"

Noel did not need his script to answer that. Every waking moment he was planning and dreaming how he would use Paul. There were, however, sacrifices to be made, and he would not sacrifice his finished work.

"I could finish with him by the end of the week. I've got, as you saw, to the point where he expects blind obedience."

"It would be quite possible to move now to the older Jonathan."

Noel tried ineffectually to keep bitterness out of his voice.

"Everything's possible. After all, it's only a picture; it isn't a matter of life and death to anybody but me that to please a stupid, conceited, jealous actor . . ."

William Dragon patted Noel's arm.

"I don't like it any more than you do, but he has it in writing that the childhood sequences will not be made too much of." He was silent a moment thinking. "I shall telephone him now. I shall say I have seen for the first time the rushes of Jonathan's early childhood. I shall suggest that I felt that too much was being expected of the small boy we had engaged, and that he will finish this week, and you would like to start young Robert's sequences on Monday."

Noel's face was white.

"Tell him any damn lie you like. I only hope I don't murder young Robert Dram."

William Dragon went on quietly:

"If Robert Dram starts on Monday there will be no need to cut any of the stuff we saw to-day." Noel turned to go back to the set. "And, Noel, I'll have all the whole grapevine working to find a good story to star a little boy, and you shall direct it."

That evening Doris went to see Emma. Emma was in her kitchen, preparing supper. At one time she would have snatched off her apron and entertained Doris in the front room, now she merely nodded to a chair by the kitchen table.

"Sit down, dear, and tell me all about it."

Doris lit a cigarette before she spoke.

"I don't know where to start. First of all, we've got a child-wonder in the family." Emma moved, but Doris stopped her. "You know me, I'm not one to get excited about a child actor, but Paul's quite extraordinary. I only saw things called rushes—which means all they have filmed without cutting and tidying up—and even in that stage I was amazed. He moved me, he frightened me, and he horrified me. It's a beastly story; it shows, I believe, how a thorough-going scoundrel became like that, through things that happened when he was a child."

"How is Paul?"

Doris got up to look for something to use as an ashtray.

"I'm out of my depth in all this. I think, from what I've picked up from Jimmie, the kids at school have bullied and teased him; you know what beasts kids are, and you know how Ruth spoiled him. I don't believe any of this nonsense she talks about neurotic infantilism and compensation and all the rest of it; I think he may have been getting an ordinary inferiority complex, which is a thing which needs seeing to. If he was, this film ought to have cured him."

Emma thickened her gravy.

"That's good, dear; and it'll soon be over; and then Paul can go back to school and Ruth needn't worry about him any more."

Doris laughed.

"It's not as simple as all that. Ruth's worried stiff about him. It's making her ill; she fainted when she saw the rushes. In the film the child has to believe that inanimate things like clocks can talk, and obey his orders, and it seems, to help this idea along, they've played up the idea in the studio, until Paul thinks everything can move and talk. I wasn't there, but I gather he screamed his head off because farm animals, which Mr. Dragon—who's the big shot of the film company—gave him, wouldn't move when he told them to."

Emma smiled.

"He'll get over that. All children have their fancies, but they pass. In the boys' bedroom I had wallpaper with silver lattice and roses; very pretty it was. Andrew thought that of a night time he climbed through the lattice and walked in a rose-garden."

"Andrew!"

"Yes, you wouldn't think it now, would you? I let it pass until I thought we'd had enough of it; then I changed the wallpaper to a plain one. It was getting dirty, anyway."

Doris looked with affection at Emma's plump back view. Had anything ever seemed complex to her?

"I don't think this film business is going to end as easily as you think. I would guess that when the film is shown Paul causes quite a sensation."

"He need never know, dear."

"I wonder. Children are awful snobs. They are just as quick to lionise a child as they are to give it an inferiority complex. I think Ruth is scared stiff about what she's let him in for. She looks wretched. One thing, rumour had it before we left that Paul's part would finish this week. That's at least two weeks sooner than Ruth expected. Somebody called 'stills', who wanted a picture of Paul with his farm animals, told her. He said Robert Dram was called for Monday; Robert Dram is Nicholas Dram's son, who plays Jonathan at about twelve, I think. If he's coming Paul's part will be finished, 'stills' thought; he seemed very surprised."

Emma brought her saucepan to the table and strained her gravy into a sauceboat.

"Isn't that splendid news? I am glad; so will Dad be." Doris got up.

"He's late, isn't he?"

Emma's face was non-committal.

"He's seeing George about something."

Doris leant on the table.

"Is he? What are you plotting?"

Emma raised innocent eyes.

"Me, dear! I'm just an old stupid; I never plot things. Dad's the clever one. But I don't think plot's a nice word—" She broke off."

"Oh, Doris, if Ruth has finished having to go to those studios I wonder if you could all come here on Sunday. There may be something nice to tell. Dad would like you all to hear it. Could you arrange for someone to stay with the children and you and Andrew come to supper?"

Doris laid a hand on Emma's. Emma looked up in surprise; it was unlike Doris to be demonstrative.

"Is it Anna's compensation?"

"You wait till Dad tells you."

"And has the doctor got something to do with it?" Emma's eyes twinkled.

"The doctor! Whatever put that idea in your head?" Doris moved to the door.

"A window at Littleton's looks over the garden of 'The Green Man'. I always wondered what my mother-in-law was doing there."

Emma looked distressed.

"Now, dear, don't be too clever. You forget you saw me. You don't want to spoil pleasure on Sunday, do you?"

"No, and I wouldn't mind giving pleasure to Mum-Tring if I knew what would give her pleasure."

Emma's head shot up.

"Wouldn't you, dear? Oh, Doris, you are kind! Funny, and only a short while back I was scared of you."

"What's it to be?"

Emma laughed.

"As if you didn't know! You make Dad happy, and have your children christened."

For a moment Doris wavered; that was indeed a giving-in; then she looked at the eagerness and hope on Emma's face.

"All right; but remember it's a present to you."

"Tell him on Sunday, and don't mention me, will you, there's a love?"

Doris gave a nod of acceptance and left the kitchen. She was surprised at how easy the giving-in had been. It was queer, but in a way she was glad. It was pleasant to think of telling Andrew her news. How his face would shine, like Jimmie's when she gave him a treat. She would not confess it, but she would be glad her children could go to church with their friends. She would never force them, but sometimes lately she had wondered if a church background was not rather a good thing. She had never had it, but Emma had.

Noel had a talk with Ruth the next day. He told her that he would not need Paul after Saturday. He did not embroider that, but left it as a bald statement; she could make what she liked of this change of plans. Almost certainly studio gossip would give her something approximating to the truth. He had not been prepared for her reaction. He knew she was an unusual film child's mother, but that his news could make her look as if the sun were shining on her face surprised him.

"Oh, Mr. Water! Am I pleased! Why, that's just wonderful news."

He sat down beside her.

"You don't like film work for him, do you?"

Ruth struggled to be fair.

"Maybe, finishing now, it may have been just what he needed; but I was kind of scared of any more of it."

Noel got up and roamed round the dressing-room. He spoke out loud, more to himself than to her.

"I'll never have such material again. The critics will say he's a genius; he isn't, he's a very sensitive, directable little boy. If I'm remembered for nothing else, I'll be remembered for those sequences . . . likely as not he won't be able to act when he's older."

"There's no reason why he should, Mr. Water. Neither his father nor I would wish it for him."

Noel swung round to her.

"My dear Mrs. Tring. Don't you know in the least what you've let yourself in for? Don't you know what you've signed! The Rose of England Film Corporation have an option on your son, and they'll take it up, unless somebody prevents them, and they'll ruin him. I saw your face to-day when Bill Dragon told Paul he was going to be a very important little boy. That's just the beginning. Soon he will be petted and lionised and asked for his autograph, and you will have the pleasure of watching him lapping it up, taking delight in it all, posing, expecting to be recognised . . ." He stopped. "What's the matter? You aren't going to do another faint, are you?"

Ruth pulled herself together.

"No. I haven't been feeling very well. It's worrying about Paul, I guess. You scared me. They can't make him act in another picture, can they?"

Noel started pacing again.

"They could. They will. Even at this minute the feelers are out looking for a great story for him for me to direct. He'll be starred. He'll be rich. Don't you want him to be rich?"

"No. I just want him to grow up a fine man."

Noel paused.

"I expect I'm behaving like a lunatic, but I'm going to help you. I said the company would take up an option unless somebody prevented them. I shall prevent them. I shall go to Bill Dragon and advise him that I think Paul's talent is just a flash in the pan; that alone would not stop him, but I'll say I don't want to direct him again. I think that will do it."

"Why are you doing this? It's wonderfully kind."

"I'm not sure. Partly it's true. I don't think I'll ever get that same quality from him again, and partly I've got a conscience. Paul is the last type to come well out of being poodle-faked around." Noel stopped and picked up Ruth's hands. "As well, I admire his mother. The only mother I ever met who had a chance of a great film career for her son, and for his soul's sake said 'No.'"

Emma and Dad-Tring always went to church on Sunday evenings, so Sunday supper was not until eight. Though it was late for them to eat, and though Dad was fortified for the ordeal of fasting until eight by eggs with his tea, it was by custom a solid meal. There was a large pie at one end of the table and a cold chicken at the other. Large bowls of lettuce, water-cress, radishes and onions were within the reach of every hand. On the sideboard were the sweets. The centre-piece was the trifle, for Emma was famous for her trifles. As well there was a fruit tart, jam tarts, and a cold rice pudding. Beside Emma was the teapot; all the Trings drank tea during the meal, but when it was over the men had beer and the women were offered port.

It was not until the major eating was over that Dad made his announcement. He was fond of an occasion, and he made it clear this was one by thumping on the table for silence.

"I've got a bit of news you may all like to hear. It was brought to my notice by the doctor that old General P. wouldn't be able to stand again for Parliament. 'D.T.,' the doctor said to me, 'I'm off to see old General P. If I tell him what I think I should tell him—that he must give up—would you cough up the money for that clever son of yours, George, to fight a by-election?'"

Anna hardly dared to believe what she had heard. "Stand for Parliament! George!"

Dad nodded proudly.

"Why not? Clever as paint your George is, young woman, and though I shouldn't tell you, the doctor said you'd look very pretty as the Member's wife."

Anna turned to Emma. So this was what she had meant; but it was better, far better than she could have dreamt. Member's wife! That would put all the snooty fools in their places; they would fall over each other to entertain their Member's wife.

Emma saw that Anna was going to thank her. She stopped her.

"I think it's a wonderful idea, George."

George was quietly happy.

"If I get elected."

Dad gave a snort.

"Elected. Of course you'll get elected. A son of mine, backed by my friends, will walk in. Besides, it will be popular; the gentry have been saying for a long time we needed new blood in the Conservative Party, and nothin's so likely to increase our membership as havin' someone like you—just an ordinary town chap—standin'."

George turned to Anna.

"I couldn't tell you before. Dad said it was to be a secret until this evening."

Dad was pleased with himself.

"That's right. I'm goin' to pay the expenses, and I reckon that gives me the right to tell the news. It will be all over the town to-morrow. Old General P. applied for the Chiltern Hundreds yesterday."

Emma smiled at Anna.

"I think you ought to give Dad a big hug. He's been thinking George needed a wider life, and you too. He's a clever one, isn't he?"

Doris, with an amused eye, watched Anna get up and put her arms round Dad's neck and press her lips to his cheek. Silly old man! He looked so pleased. Someone would have to see there was no backsliding from Anna. Clever old Emma had thought of this way of giving her what she wanted, and Anna must repay with affection. It was a very neat idea getting George to stand for the Conservative Party. That doddering old General had driven everybody so mad; there might have been a move to the Left if someone like George had not been selected to stand at the by-election. George was exactly what was needed. He was clever, he knew the people he would represent, his father was a most respected citizen. As a good socialist she ought to be mad with them all, but she found she wasn't. She knew in her heart that no socialist, no matter who stood, would be returned in such a Tory stronghold, and oddly she didn't much care. Careful, thoughtful George would be a good, honest Member, and that was something.

As Anna sat down, Doris got up. She went to Dad, but her eyes were on Emma. She put her arms round Dad's neck.

"This seems to be a hugging evening, and I don't see why I should be out of it." She caught Emma's eyes and held them. "You're not the only one with a bit of news. Andrew and I are having the children christened next Sunday."

In the excitement the fact that Andrew was as surprised as Dad escaped everybody except Emma. Dad was thumping the table.

"Put away the damned tea, Emma. This is an occasion. Get out the glasses. Whisky for me and the boys, and glasses of port for you girls."

Emma got up. "Give me a hand with the cups, Ruthie dear. Now, Dad, you take everybody into the front room for their drinks. I'll be along in a minute with the glasses."

In the kitchen it was only the work of a moment to pile the cups in the sink, wipe the tray and fill it with glasses. Ruth moved to pick it up. Emma stopped her.

"No, dearie, I'll take it." She took Ruth's face between her hands. "It's nice to see you again. I've missed you these last weeks."

Ruth dropped her eyes to hide that they glistened with tears.

"I'm not sure I did right. The movie business seemed to get such a hold of Paul, and maybe it hasn't helped any; he could still need compensating."

"Could he? I don't think so. I think he's going to have the best compensation, isn't he?" Ruth looked puzzled. "I know the look, dearie. You slip along to Doctor Wilks tomorrow; he'll tell you I'm right."

Ruth gazed starry-eyed at her mother-in-law.

"Well, of all the sillies . . . I've been feeling unwell and—"

Peter came in.

"Dad says, where are the glasses?"

Ruth flung her arms round him.

"Peter, I believe I've started another baby."

In bed that night, Dad, who had drunk plenty of whisky, could not stop chuckling.

"If this doesn't beat fox-huntin'. Peter thinks it was the film that did the trick."

Emma, lying on her side where she could see the outline of his face, laughed with him.

"But, mind you, it may be true. Who was the clever one who said a proper shake-up might set everything right." Dad gave another rumbling chuckle.

"Did you see them? Anna hangin' round my neck one minute and Doris the other. We won't half have a do next Sunday. For the christenin's I'll set both the boys up with savin' stamps . . . And now Ruthie and Peter havin' a baby . . . if that don't beat cock-fightin'. When I was plannin' things I never hoped to work that one."

Emma heard his laugh die away into a snore. She raised herself on her elbow and looked at him. Nice he was so pleased with himself. Everything wouldn't turn out as he planned, but it looked like smooth water ahead, and he deserved it, bless him. She softly kissed his forehead. "Sweet dreams, old dear."

THE END

FURROWED MIDDLEBROW

*titles available in paperback only

**pseudonym of Noel Streatfeild

9 781915 393302